The Dead Indian

DORIS M. DORWART

authorHOUSE®

AuthorHouse™
1663 Liberty Drive
Bloomington, IN 47403
www.authorhouse.com
Phone: 1 (800) 839-8640

Published by AuthorHouse 07/25/2018

ISBN: 978-1-5462-5053-1 (sc)
ISBN: 978-1-5462-5051-7 (hc)
ISBN: 978-1-5462-5052-4 (e)

Library of Congress Control Number: 2018908507

Print information available on the last page.

ACKNOWLEDGEMENTS

I like fairy tales. They appeal to my sense of fairness. The prince always gets the girl and the hero slays the dragon. But I have come to realize that life does not always emulate the tales I love so dearly.

Right does not always win. But, then, it all depends on what one views as *right*. As I interact with the other residents here at Longs Community, I hear such fabulous stories, heartaches, heroic deeds, and happenings that it would take me several lifetimes to capture them all. Perhaps some of my friends will not agree with the decisions made by my characters in this story. So, won't you come along—no peeking at the ending—and then let me know what you would have done.

Thank you, my friends, for the encouragement you give me each and every day. Without you, I would lack the strength and the desire to keep on writing. I hope you enjoy my quirky characters. You never know, perhaps they might move in here with us some day!

PROLOGUE

The silver-haired man was hardly visible in the early evening dusk as he sat on a bench near the Timber Run River. He loved the river—it always mesmerized him, soothed his soul, and somehow reaffirmed his self-assurance. However, now there were important decisions that he had to make—putting them off was no longer an option. Today, his doctor informed him that he probably had less than twenty-four months to live. His vast financial empire—all that he had built over the years—must be turned over to his nephews. While he had raised them from the time they were teenagers and tried to teach them the skills necessary to be successful in the business world, he wasn't sure that they were ready for such an awesome responsibility. Flipping through his Bible, he stopped when he came to a verse in Ecclesiastes he had highlighted in Ecclesiastes. *As for every man to whom God had given riches and wealth, and given him power to eat it, to receive his heritage and rejoice in his labor—this is a gift of God.*

He had wealth; more than most men. He knew how to make money. While he hoped that he had prepared his heirs properly, he was a bit concerned about their private lives. Entanglements outside of business could easily destroy the very soul of his empire. They needed to understand that they had to achieve two major goals: (1) to increase the holdings of the business, and (2) to make certain that no one or anything sullied the name of the company's founder. They needed to be strong stewards of his reputation and his financial empire. He wondered if they were hardened enough to direct and govern his precious enterprise. After all, there were times when it had been necessary to be ruthless to protect the family.

Stroking his beard, his eyes followed the current and eddies of the river as they moved by rapidly. What to do. What to do. Then, it dawned on him. He should hire someone to gather information on his heirs before he decided who got what. Now that he had a solution, he could relax. He sat back on the bench and watched a small whirlpool swallow a leaf. The river had never let him down—now his heirs must do the same. A line from a poem by Eric Burdon ran through his mind: *There are so many times in one's life, when one feels he has nothing to offer. But, no, my river had not run dry.*

CHAPTER 1

MARY JO LEANED heavily on the bathroom sink. Her head was hanging down, so she could not see her face. She didn't want to look at herself—a God-fearing woman—who did the unthinkable. There were no excuses. Nothing, or no one to blame it on; just herself. In spite of this, her mind went back to this afternoon. Slowly, she forced herself to accept what she had done, but the problem looming on the horizon was that she wanted to see him again. Slowly, his name rolled off her tongue—Darius.

Without looking in the mirror, she turned and sat on the edge of the tub. She reached for her bath salts and sprinkled them over the mat. Turning on the water full force, she watched as little pebbles created mounds of white suds. When they were almost even with the edge of the tub, she turned the water off and climbed in. Putting a small pillow behind her head, Mary Jo leaned back and closed her eyes. His smile—his voice—his touch were all beyond her reach. Surprisingly, she had no regrets—or so she tried to tell herself.

As her thoughts shifted to Greg, however, guilt took over. She had no idea how she would be able to keep this from her husband. In the twenty-five years that they had been married, she had never experienced anything like she had this afternoon. Many years ago, her Aunt Emma had told her that having sex was the price wives had to pay for having their husbands take care of them and that she should just close her eyes and that it would soon be over. Now that she knew better, Mary Jo was even more miserable when she thought about the possibility of never being with Darius again.

Mary Jo thought it amazing that just two days before her forty-fifth birthday, she had entered a new phase of her life. What happened today had really begun months ago when Maggie Adams, director of the Cutler County Animal Rescue Association, where Mary Jo volunteered, asked her to represent the organization on the planning committee for a charity event, designed to raise money for the many special services that were at the disposal of the residents of Cutler County. She had almost turned her down since she knew that her sister-in-law, Crystal Fadden, also would be attending the meetings to represent a shelter being built for abused women and children. The sisters-in-law spent as little time as possible together, and they were perfectly happy with such an arrangement. But Maggie had pleaded, and Mary Jo had given in.

The committee had decided on a formal name for the four-day event—Sharing Talent and Inter-agency Resources Services—STAIRS. Thirty-two organizations had joined forces to strengthen the financial support needed to address the special needs of the population of Cutler County. Each organization had been adopted by a large corporation that agreed to provide not only financial support for the undertaking, but also guidance in putting together such a huge event. For their logo, they had chosen a sketch of a flight of stairs with a figure moving to the top.

When Mary Jo had arrived at the first committee meeting, she had learned that Darius Davis, of Davis Media, would be her sponsor. When she had turned to shake his hand, she had looked into his eyes and had known that something was different about this man. After casually removing his jacket and hanging it over the chair beside her, he had smiled and immediately had begun a friendly conversation. Her heart had begun beating rapidly and her hands had trembled slightly. Mary Jo had reminded herself that she was a married woman with a college-aged daughter; not a silly school girl looking for her first love. While Mary Jo had tried to take copious notes during the meeting, she had difficulty focusing on the topics at hand.

The director had explained that each charity would be responsible for holding 'show and tell' presentations that could be held at their headquarters or at other venues. He suggested lectures, interesting demonstrations, entertainment, or anything that would bring people to their event. He also had reminded the committee members that they needed to provide both free and paid events. Each person attending any paid event would receive a lottery ticket good for fantastic prizes to be awarded at a big party on the last day.

"I understand that the top prize will be a new car. Also, several fully-paid trips and lots of shopping passes will be given away. So, make sure that you plan activities for your organization that will really get your donors excited. By getting your donors to actually come into your buildings, they may be more likely to develop a sense of ownership and become genuinely excited about your mission."

When the gavel had sounded to indicate that the first meeting had come to an end, Darius had turned to her and said, "I don't know about you, but I'm starved. Perhaps you would join me for lunch. You can share the ideas you probably already have in mind to showcase the need of the animals under your care."

They had rapidly fallen into a pattern—meeting and then lunching—just the two of them. Inevitably, they had crossed a line that was now obliterated and things might never be the same for either one of them.

When the bath water began to cool, Mary Jo was brought back to the present. She got out of the tub, dried off, and stepped on the scale. She smiled when she saw 116 flashing at her—just exactly what she weighed when she was a senior in high school. With the hair dryer in one hand and her brush in the other, she quickly attended to her short, naturally wavy blonde hair.

She put her new silk pajamas on and went into the living room. The house was quiet. Greg was out of town and Beth was two hundred miles away at college. If either of them had been home, maybe her afternoon would never have happened. "Oh, great," she said out loud, "you can't live with your guilt so go ahead and blame your husband and your daughter."

Although her home was beautiful, she hated it. It was all Greg's idea to buy a place in Melody Park, the area where people who had *made it* called home. Since Greg was seldom at home, Mary Jo was surprised when he had insisted on purchasing such an expensive property. She missed her old condo, located just a few blocks from her best friend, Cindy. Greg was proud of his six-figure salary and fully expected to take over his uncle's investment and insurance firm with its many branches. Uncle Roger also owned real estate all over the country. Despite his wealth, Mary Jo despised him. He always made it apparent that he thought Greg had married beneath his station, and he enjoyed keeping Greg on a string just like a puppet, dangling the possibility that he would own

THE DEAD INDIAN

a financial empire someday. Greg never discussed business with her, so she had no idea what he was responsible for and where he went on his frequent business trips.

When Mary Jo would ask her husband about the mission of the Fadden Foundation, he would begrudgingly respond that the work was private and could not be shared with anyone. Although he was away from home a great deal, it never had crossed her mind that he could possibly have another woman. He simply was not a sexual man. His lovemaking, at best, was mechanical, almost obligatory. One time, when she had made a suggestion when he was on top of her, he had become irate and had loudly responded that he didn't want a whore for a wife.

She had absolutely no idea what Greg earned. Mary Jo had gotten used to his secrecy about their finances and merely took it for granted that Greg didn't want, nor needed, any advice from her. When she had suggested that she seek some type of employment, he had gotten very upset and had forbidden her to bring the topic up again. She thought of Greg as a modern-day King Midas—sitting in his castle, stacking up his golden coins and possessions, one by one.

CHAPTER 2

Twenty-five years before

I T WAS A lovely, early fall day and Mary Jo was going to be married. Her mother was in the kitchen preparing a small breakfast buffet for some of Greg's relatives. However, Roger Fadden was not among them—just one more way to remind others that he was against his nephew Greg's choice for a wife.

Cindy, Mary Jo's Maid of Honor, was sprawled across the bed, filing her nails and enjoying the slight breeze that was floating into the open third-floor bedroom window. They could hear the hubbub from the busy street below. Cindy went to the window to see who was arriving.

"How come Greg's uncle isn't coming?" Cindy questioned.

"He doesn't approve of me. I guess I'm just too poor for his taste," Mary Jo said as she checked her lipstick.

"Doesn't that make you angry?" Cindy asked.

"Sure it does. But some of Greg's relatives on his mom's side sort of make up for that. He's looney. Greg only works for his uncle, but Roger wants to make all Greg's personal decisions. I thought he might fire Greg, but that didn't happen."

The two sat quietly for a while. Suddenly, Mary Jo began pacing. "That Roger Fadden makes me so angry. Just who does he think he is to look down his nose at me?" Punching her right fist into her left hand, she suddenly stopped pacing and said, "I know, I'm going to get back at him."

"How do you plan on doing that?" Cindy asked.

"I'm not going to get married. I'm going to say that Greg Fadden isn't good enough to marry *me*," an excited Mary Jo declared.

Cindy froze. "Say what? What do you mean you're not getting married? You've been planning this day for over a year."

"I know that. That will rattle Roger Fadden's cage!" Mary Jo said firmly.

"Hold it. I'll go get your mom," Cindy said as she hurried down the stairs.

Her mother stomped up the stairs and was breathing hard as she got to the top of the stairs and faced her daughter. Mary Jo shuddered.

"Cindy, will you please wait downstairs. I need to have a discussion with my daughter," her mom ordered. "Mary Jo, if this is another one of your mind-changing ideas, I want you to know that I don't have time for such nonsense."

"Mom, this is not nonsense. I really don't want to get married today or any other day," Mary Jo said as she clenched her teeth together. "At least not to Greg."

"What!" her mom thundered. "You have cold feet. A lot of brides do. But remember, young lady, your father and I have put out a lot of money for this day, and we will not allow you to make fools out of us. You can't go through life changing your mind at every corner."

"I don't do that, Mom," Mary Jo said angrily as she looked down at the floor.

"Oh no? How about the time you wanted to be a cheerleader? You went to two sessions and then you quit the squad. Then, you joined the chorus. That was another activity you quit. Oh, and how about having your father and I drive you all over creation, looking at colleges, only to have you decide that college was not for you. I'm not having this, young lady. You can't find a better man than Greg Fadden. He's a polite young man who comes from a wealthy family. I don't know what more you could want. The boy's been in love with you since junior high."

"Greg's uncle is wealthy, not Greg."

"No. You listen to me, Miss Know-it-All. Grow up. You made a commitment and I expect you to follow through. Cindy, come up here," her mom called out sharply. "Help Mary Jo get ready. We *are* having a wedding today. I have had enough of this falderal. I don't want to hear another word from you, young lady." And with that, she stormed down the stairway, slamming the door behind her.

Three hours later the wedding had gone on as planned.

❧ CHAPTER 3 ❧

CINDY HAD JUST finished using the steamer on the kitchen floor. When she put her cleaning tools back in the closet, she headed for the comfortable leather lounge chair that her husband had bought her last week. The little card that he had attached to the chair read, *"An early anniversary present."* Russ never forgot any of their special days. And, even though he was on the road a lot, somehow he had always managed to get something delivered to her. As she ran her hands over the lovely beige chair, she smiled. Without bothering to remove her apron, she stretched her long legs out and reached for the remote control so she could watch Dr. Phil, one of her favorite shows.

She had been disappointed that she hadn't reached Mary Jo again and was beginning to feel sorry for herself. For the past few weeks, Mary Jo simply hadn't had enough time for her no matter the activity. Cindy tried to remember if, by chance, she had said something or had done something that would cause Mary Jo to ignore her again and again. When Mary Jo had first moved to Melody Park, Cindy had been concerned that her friend might take up with women in that area and forget all about her. However, she and Mary Jo had remained *best buds*; but now, their relationship was not as warm and fuzzy as it had been. She wondered if Mary Jo was drifting away on purpose.

When she realized that Dr. Phil was going to deal with a gang member, she turned to the music channel. She couldn't stand to see another young person, who had their whole life in front of them, give one excuse after another for their anti-social behavior. Cindy had no patience for people who were just plain stupid.

As beautiful music began to float through the air, Cindy started to feel more like herself. But it wasn't long before her thoughts drifted back to Mary Jo. Something must be wrong with her friend. Perhaps Mary Jo had developed some type of medical problem—something she just didn't want to share with Cindy. If it had been a marital problem, Mary Jo would have talked that over with her. However, since Cindy never thought too much of Greg, Cindy's tendency was to accuse him unjustly. Oh, he was nice looking, had a good job, and made lots of money, but he hadn't a clue that his wife was not very happy.

Mary Jo was the person who had helped Cindy through her two miscarriages. While Russ would hold her and kiss her forehead to comfort her, he simply could not put his feelings into words. It was Mary Jo, who was able to get her to look through the dark abyss in order to go on with her life. And, that upset Cindy because Mary Jo always knew what to say and do whenever Cindy experienced disappointments—and there had been a few. She had longed for a child, but she now accepted the fact that that would never happen. Fortunately, Cindy found a way to use her maternal side by working with the pre-school program at her church. Since she began helping the little ones there, Cindy discovered an outlet for her urge to be a *mother hen*.

Gradually, she had accepted her fate. Cindy, however, was grateful that she had Russ. He truly loved her. She never had had any doubt about his loyalty—even while he was on the road for days at a time. She had fallen in love with him on the day that she met him at the county fair. He was at least a foot taller than she, but he was not awkward as he shook her hand politely and smiled at her. He liked to tease her by saying that she was vertically challenged. Surprising herself, she had given him her phone number as they stood beside the merry-go-round. From there on, it was history.

As she looked around her living room, she spied several gifts that Russ had bought her. Some of them were just trinkets, probably from some gas station gift shop, while others obviously were far more expensive. Deep in her heart she knew that Russ would lay down his life for her—a glorious warmth spread throughout her body. She thought about the gift that she planned on giving Russ for Christmas and smiled. Winston Worthington, a prize-winning local artist, had agreed to paint a portrait of Russ's mother and dad from an old, faded sepia photo. She was looking forward to seeing the finished work next week. Russ had worked tirelessly over the years, never turning down a job to drive for hours and hours, to provide for her and to help pay for the medical needs of his parents as they lingered in the nursing home. Russ took it hard when his father died in February and then, just six weeks later, his mother succumbed to Parkinson's.

In addition to her commitment to the pre-school program, Cindy filled her days by using her ability as a seamstress. She was a genius at altering clothing for women and even took on the challenge of outfitting brides and their attendants. Russ was very proud of her accomplishments and would often brag about her to anyone who struck up a conversation with him—even people he met on the road and would probably never see again. After talking with Russ, a person had no doubt that he was crazy about her. She was his best friend and soul mate.

Reaching into her apron pocket, she pulled out a ribbon which she used to create a pony tail with her long, chestnut-brown hair. Mary Jo would occasionally recommend that Cindy cut her hair and would show her pictures of the latest hair fashions. While she had her hair trimmed from time to time, Cindy knew that Russ liked her hair long. So that was that.

Cindy picked up her cell phone and placed another call to her best friend. The call immediately went to the message box. With a heavy heart, and too disappointed to leave a message, Cindy hung up. Even when Mary Jo was at work, she used to answer her cell phone. Once again, Mary Jo was out somewhere—somewhere where she didn't want to be bothered. Cindy closed her eyes. Perhaps the handwriting was on the wall. Maybe, Cindy thought, Mary Jo just doesn't want me in her life anymore.

CHAPTER 4

Roger Fadden was in his usual place, seated behind his immense, ornate, walnut desk with mounds of paperwork in front of him. He knew it was time to make decisions that he had been putting off for a long time. He had already made out his will as far as some inheritances were concerned. He bequeathed a tidy sum to Teresa, his housekeeper, for her many years of devoted service. He hadn't made up his mind what he wanted to do for all of his employees. He needed to mull that over. Last week, he had announced that his older nephew, Greg, would be responsible for the investment side of his business as well as the Fadden Foundation. His other nephew, Joshua, would be placed in charge of the insurance companies and the real estate that he owned. However, he was a bit concerned whether the two of them could continue to move his business model forward so that the company would retain its position as the largest investment and insurance firm in the state. He wanted his name to live on.

He admitted to himself that it had sometimes been difficult to hang on to his religious beliefs, while making lucrative business decisions. Roger was a shrewd businessman. His fellow parishioners believed that he upheld the tenets of his church in his business and in his personal life—however, they were not aware that Roger believed that business was another matter. He believed that what one must do to earn money should not be measured using the same yardstick. One had to be shrewd to make money and smart enough to understand how to do it without sharing all of it with the government. He had to be certain that his nephews would do the same thing. While they appeared to be doing an excellent job with the Fadden Foundation, he had to be certain that they could keep their spouses under control as well. A life-long bachelor, Roger didn't trust women. They didn't have the backbone or the intelligence to know how to handle investors. He often had wished that neither one of his nephews had married. But they had, so Roger had to learn how to work around the two wives.

While Roger owned several other companies, his powerful investment and insurance empires were the most valuable assets that he had created. He could recite the date and time when he had opened each branch office. Roger has been making shrewd deals all his business life. The disappearance of his partner was a necessary "shrewd deal" many years before. With all the restrictions that the government placed on employers, it was difficult to hire and fire people that did not live up to his expectations. However, the one thing he could do before he made his final decisions was to have his private investigator conduct an in-depth examination of both Greg and Joshua. While on the surface the two men appeared to lead Christian lives, one could never be too careful when it came to turning over millions of dollars to someone else—even relatives.

Roger always had been skeptical about his nephews' wives. Joshua's wife, Crystal, was constantly in the newspaper, heading up this and that charity drive. Whenever she laughed, she created a sound that surely could wake the dead. He felt that she wore too much makeup and it sickened him. She also had an annoying habit of playing with her hair all the time like a little girl. Mary Jo, Greg's wife, was just as annoying. Whenever she was in Roger's company, she looked completely bored. She had a habit of always looking around the room as if she were waiting for someone more important to arrive.

Women just had too many bad habits. He had managed to ignore them quite successfully. Along the way, there had been several that had set their caps for him, but he was too smart for such treachery. But Beth, Greg's daughter, was different. Roger had already set aside a special legacy for her. She called him Papa Roger, and he loved it. Not only was she a beauty, but she also was extremely intelligent. She sent him emails to let him know what was happening at college and always signed them with love.

He leaned back in his chair, adjusted his tired frame, and allowed his mind to think of his only love. Oh, it had happened so very long ago. He was just a boy in high school when he met the sister of one of his friends. He was instantly smitten. When she had smiled at him, his knees had shaken. He hadn't known much about the intricacies of flirting, but he had felt that, even though she was much older than he was, she had been romantically interested in him. Then, just like the wind in the willows, she had disappeared. It was then that he decided to build a wall around his heart—no woman would ever leave him again.

Picking up a framed photo of Beth, Roger ran his hand over the glass. He needed to guide her in some way so she would want to follow in his footsteps. He had very few women in administrative positions in his company, but Beth could prove to be the exception. He would wait and see which way she went when she graduated from college. Perhaps he should make arrangements for her to start working with Joshua in a branch office, allowing her to learn the business from the bottom up.

Roger had already made certain that Otto, whom he now regarded as a faithful charge, would have a place to live. He had made arrangements with the Riverton Personal Care Community that when Roger's time arrived, Otto would be able to move into a small apartment. Several years ago, Roger had hired Otto to do some yard work. He had connected to the man instantly even though it had been obvious that he was special. Otto had brought back memories of Roger's younger brother, Parke—he, too. had been special. Roger had loved his brother and had taken care of him until his death at age twelve. After all, that's what strong families do.

While Otto could be considered special—and probably rode that little yellow bus to school when he was a child— Otto was faithful and always followed Roger's orders. When Roger had offered to give him some household items, he had discovered that Otto was living in a cardboard box under the bridge on the outside of town. While Roger was not known for his compassion, something had encouraged him to make a home for Otto in the basement of his home. Besides, his fellow church councilmen would give him accolades for being so generous. Otto had had a great time painting the basement walls and hanging little curtains at the doorway to his new abode. Now, Roger, and the rest of the Faddens, looked upon Otto as extended family.

Then, yesterday, Otto had asked Roger if he could get a dog. Roger's first instinct had been to say a loud resounding "NO", but when he had taken a good look at Otto's hopeful smile, he surprisingly had given the man permission to get a dog.

"Otto," he had said firmly, "no cats, no creepy crawly

things, just a dog—a male dog. And, not one of those dogs that yaps all the time. You must walk him every day and keep him healthy. Talk with Mary Jo at the animal shelter. She can give you the name of a good vet. You must make certain he gets all his shots and keep him groomed. Have any bills sent to me. Oh, one more thing: I don't ever want to see any dog poop in the yard. And, never let him in my kitchen—if he does, you will have to get rid of him."

"I'll get a good dog," Otto had assured Roger. "One that likes me and will listen to what I say."

"How are you going to be sure of that?" Roger had asked.

"Oh, I'll know," Otto had said with a smile on his face.

Still recalling the conversation, Roger stood up and opened the blind. He stood there, stroking his short, well-trimmed beard. No wonder the pioneers called this town Riverton. On either side of dark waters, greenery covered the banks. In the distance, he could see the mountains lined tightly against one another, like an impenetrable army, protecting all who lived within their shadow. He hoped that he would still be around next fall since that was when the mountains would display a wide range of colors. He looked out over Hemlock Street and, as usual, was mesmerized at the way Timber Run never ceased flowing. A river could be powerful when it needed to be, but also peaceful and serene, hiding its power from everyone, but always ready to overwhelm and claim whatever it wanted. One could easily see the life-giving waters; however, what was underneath, in the darkness—away from the sun and the light—could be frightening. Roger shook his head. He, too, was like a river. He had power—more than most men. Sometimes he used that power for good, while at other times, for business purposes, he had to be almost cruel in order to maintain his status. He always felt that the difference between success and failure, in business and in life in general, was the ability to use power at the right time, regardless of what others thought. He had to be prudent and do this right. He needed to order an investigation on his nephews and their wives and it needed to be done right now. Then, and only then, would he make his changes legal.

Just as he turned to sit down again, he felt those scary shooting pains. He could no longer afford the luxury of time. He needed to get his affairs in order. In his business dealings, from time to time, Roger had had to negotiate with people with unsavory reputations. He reached for the little black notebook he kept in his breast pocket. Oh, what stories this little book could tell. If he ever needed the kind of services that these people provided, he would not hesitate to call them. Then, he glanced down at his bottom desk drawer. The only way it could be opened was to push on the forehead of the carving that always reminded Roger of an Indian. Some time soon, he would have to destroy the paperwork and the special phones that he kept hidden there. Leaning down, he ran his fingers over the carving, paused for a minute, and then put pressure on the right spot. Almost silently, the drawer popped open. He picked up one of the phones.

"Henry, Roger here...Yes, I know...Fine...No, I don't care where you begin, just get started...No,.No, not that, just the nephews and their wives...We'll talk about the other matter a bit later...Yes, I know...No, we don't have to meet just yet...I might need your special delivery work before too long...Yes, quite profitable...No, we cannot meet at the office...Now get busy and try to be finished before the end of January."

Roger was no sissy, or so he had thought, but just as he hung up, the pains returned. But now, as he grabbed the side of his desk to steady himself—when reality came calling—he was close to breaking down. He was determined that until he died, he would protect his reputation with every breath he had. *Roger Fadden will be eulogized as an astute businessman with a pristine reputation. No one must ever solve the mystery of the dead Indian—but that was so long ago and apparently no one cares anymore. And, after all, it could have been just an unfortunate accident. David had to slay Goliath—my Goliath just didn't appear in the Bible.*

⊰⊱ CHAPTER 5 ⊰⊱

WHEN OTTO GOT dressed in the morning, he wanted to make certain that he looked good. Picking out his favorite blue and white checkered shirt and his newest pair of jeans, he quickly put them on and then stood for a minute or two admiring himself in the floor-length mirror. He was going to get a dog today—a very special occasion. Grabbing the new jacket he bought with his very own money that he earned sweeping sidewalks along the shopping area, he took one last look in the mirror and hurried out the door. While it was an eight-block walk to the Cutler County Animal Rescue Association, he covered the distance quickly. He was excited.

As he opened the door to the association's office and heard the dogs barking, his heart began to beat faster. He spotted Mary Jo, one of his very favorite people. She always talked to him and that made him feel good. Others in town just ignored him. Otto understood that he was not very smart, but he had learned in church to love everyone, and he knew that meant even those who were not nice to him. But, sometimes it was difficult.

"Hello, Otto. I'm glad to see you. Are you here to walk some dogs again?" Mary Jo said as she closed her laptop.

"I want a dog," Otto said proudly. "One for my very own. Roger said I can have a dog, but it must be a boy dog. I know you have some back there," Otto said as he pointed to the door that led to the kennel.

Mary Jo called over her shoulder. "Sandy, will you please cover the phones while I help Otto? Otto, let's you and I sit over there so we can fill out the paper work."

"I'm not good at reading stuff," Otto said nervously.

"That's okay, Otto, I'll help you with that."

"Roger said he will pay for the dog. Mary Jo, do dogs cost lots of money?"

Just as she was about to answer, the front door opened. She was surprised to see Mitch McCabe, owner of *Eliza's Animal Sanctuary*, a private facility located two miles outside of town, leading a strange-looking dog he had on a leash.

"Well, well. Who do we have here?" Mary Jo said, chuckling as she got a closer look at the dog.

"This is Walter. As you can plainly see, he's not a beauty," Mitch offered as he released the dog from the leash.

Walter, a medium-sized mutt, reminded Mary Jo of a dog she once saw in a junkyard. His curly brown and black hair looked as if he had not been groomed in a long time. A strange kink in his tail made a funny sight from the rear. His ears appeared to be set at different angles making him appear to be standing sideways. As if Walter didn't have enough strikes against him, he only had one eye. He truly was a dog that only a mother could love.

Mary Jo and Mitch watched in amazement as Walter immediately ran over to Otto and sat on his lap. Otto was thrilled. He put his arms around Walter, who could not stop licking Otto's face.

Otto looked at Walter carefully. "Why does he only have one eye?"

"Well, Otto, some bad people owned Walter before and they were mean to him," Mitch explained.

"Did they dig his eye out?" Otto asked on the verge of crying.

"A couple of weeks ago, I found Walter stuffed in a little box in my driveway. He was almost lifeless. Blood was trickling down from his eye and running into his mouth. I suspect that a man, who owns several pit bulls, was holding dog fights somewhere up in the mountains. Walter was probably used as a bait dog for the fights. You see, Otto, a dog not trained to fight, would be tossed into the fighting area with agitated pit bulls. Walter was no match for them, and they just about ripped him apart. But, somehow, he survived."

"That's bad," Otto said as the tears fell. "How could anyone do such an ugly thing?"

"Fortunately, my helpers and I nursed him back to health and he seems to have adapted to having only one eye. When I discovered how lovable Walter was, I thought perhaps Mary Jo might be able to find him a home," Mitch explained. "However, it appears that that might have already happened," Mitch said.

"Otto, would you like to take Walter out to the turn out area for a while?" Mary Jo asked.

Otto immediately jumped up and hurried out the door with Walter at his heels.

"Wow," Mitch said, "I wish I could find homes for all my throw-away animals this quickly."

"Mitch, I just thought of something. Would you like to join our charity event we call STAIRS? Have you heard about this cooperative effort?" Mary Jo asked.

As Mitch slid out of his old leather jacket and laid it over a chair, Mary Jo became aware that he was an exceedingly well-built man. It was obvious that he took care of himself.

"I read about it in the paper, but I wasn't sure that my place would be eligible to participate. I get along mainly on donations. I inherited a farm of sixty acres, along with a few buildings, from my parents. My place is named after my mom who loved animals, especially the handicapped and the doomed. So, when I decided the land wasn't worth farming any longer, I decided to open a sanctuary and take care of those types of animals. But I could certainly use more financial help. I often find animals that someone doesn't want any longer stuffed in crates or chained to my fence post. Word has gotten around that I take in any unwanted animals."

As Mary Jo listened to Mitch, she couldn't help but admire his dedication and devotion to animals. "I'll get in touch with Darius Davis—he's our corporate advisor for the event—and arrange a meeting to get you in the loop as quickly as possible."

Otto and Walter came rushing back into the office. "Mary Jo, I want him and he wants me," he almost shouted as he pointed to Walter.

Mary Jo wasn't sure that Roger would approve of such a sad-looking dog being part of his household. "Let me make some calls, Otto, and I'll see what I can do. Mitch, if you have a few more minutes, I can explain where we are in the planning process for STAIRS. I'll be right back."

Mitch knew that he would wait. He had seen the wedding ring on Mary Jo's hand. Nonetheless, she was a nice person and the two of them might be able to work together to help their animals. Anyway, she had the most beautiful eyes and she smelled good, too.

Mary Jo went into the next room and called Roger to make certain that Walter would be well received. When she returned, she said, "Otto, guess what? Walter now belongs to you."

CHAPTER 6

C RYSTAL WAS RUNNING late. She was headed for the opening of the new women's center that would serve as a safe house for victims of domestic abuse. Joshua never objected to any of the causes which always seemed to need her assistance and for that she was grateful. In fact, he had told her that his Uncle Roger was proud of her involvement in the community. While she really loved her charity work, she mostly wanted to keep Uncle Roger happy. But, she would much rather serve on a more prestigious committee like the Women's Symphony Association. Being around abused women with their crying babies, worked on her nerves. However, the publicity was good and her photograph was in the paper almost every week. Furthermore, Senator Althouse was very involved in the shelter and Crystal had the opportunity to be around him quite frequently.

She and her husband had been living separate lives for a long time. They had agreed to be partners—he would work and earn the money and she would continue to get her monthly checks. Crystal was willing to do anything it took to help Joshua succeed. She thrived on getting noticed and being recognized on the society pages. She always was invited to all the better parties and was personally familiar with most of the *movers and shakers* in Riverton. And, even if it meant that she had to continue to live in the same house with Joshua, as long as she could maintain her status in the community, she was willing to do it until something better came along.

Checking her makeup in the rearview mirror, while she waited for the light to turn, Crystal was pleased with what she saw. Her shoulder-length black hair formed an ideal frame for her oval-shaped face. She was ready to be recognized as the wife of an extremely wealthy man. Her sister-in-law, Mary Jo, on the other hand, certainly was not classy enough to mingle with the upper crowd. How that woman could tolerate being around all that barking and the smell! Imagine trying to wear something nice at the facility. And, the press never covered any social events at the kennels with photos. She had seen Mary Jo at the shelter wearing a flannel shirt and jeans. And, oh, those shoes she wore—she might as well be working in a cow barn. Ugh! Why she couldn't have gotten involved in something more lady-like was a mystery. Crystal had a nickname for Mary Jo—Miss Ready-wear. Crystal considered her crass. When one was trying to help one's husband in the competitive business world, one had to show the world that her husband was in full command.

Crystal parked her Mercedes. When she spied two, well-dressed women coming down the sidewalk, she opened the car door and held up her feet to make certain that they spotted the Sammy-red bottoms of her shoes. Anybody, who knew anything about fashion, would recognize that her new Christian Louboutin heels cost over a thousand dollars. She rushed inside to join the others, who were assembling for the ribbon-cutting ceremony. She carried her favorite clutch—a chevron-quilted, black Yves Saint Laurent with a large YSL logo on the front. As she entered the building, she took a quick glance to see where the most important people were standing and immediately headed in their direction. Crystal managed to stand beside Senator Althouse before the press began taking pictures. She was thrilled when the senator shook her hand, looked into the video camera, and gave her credit for the completion of the center.

"Mrs. Fadden," the senator said, "we have a surprise for you. Please pull the cord on the sign above the doorway."

Crystal followed the senator's instruction. When the drape fell to the floor, and she saw that the sign said *The Crystal Fadden Center: A safe haven for women and children,* she dramatically dropped to her knees. The senator helped her up, put his arm around her, and handed her the microphone while dozens of flashbulbs went off. Crystal was glad that she had chosen her Valentino silk crepe, floral print since it would look fabulous in a photo.

For a few seconds, Crystal paused to create a dramatic effect. Then she said, "Thank you so much. I'm honored to be recognized like this, but I was not alone in this effort. I have many people to thank. We have had the Senator's support from the beginning and he willingly led the charge for us." Crystal waited while the crowd applauded. "We also have had many businesses support us in a myriad of ways. So, as you tour the facility, please take special note of the dedication plaques posted in many areas. The entire children's playroom was sponsored by Fadden Insurance and Investments. And, the nursery room was sponsored by Williams Markets. Thank you all. Enjoy your tour. Oh, by the way, the lovely holiday decorations were sponsored by several businesses and you will find their names listed on your programs."

Crystal had no intention of mentioning all of the mundane companies and groups that had donated various pieces of furniture and accoutrements. Uncle Roger would hear that she had recognized his firm, and the governor's sister would be pleased that she had given thanks to her brother's huge new market.

The ribbon-cutting ceremony could not have gone any better.

She had nailed it. Crystal was walking on air. As she stood at the mirror in the ladies room, a woman turned to her and said, "Pardon me, Mrs. Fadden, you are to be congratulated. You not only look beautiful and you move so well among all these people, but you have done something important for abused women. I so admire strong women like you."

"Thank you, my dear. And you are?"

"Oh, I'm Ellen. My husband's company donated most of the technology for this facility."

"Oh, yes, they have been a god-send in outfitting our media area," not having the slightest idea whom she meant. Quickly, she said, "I know nothing about the widgets and gidgets needed to handle our media requirements we need to run this place, but I do know that the staff is grateful for all that marvelous equipment. But, please call me Crystal," trying to bring this conversation to an end.

"Alright, Crystal."

"Well, Ellen, it's nice to make your acquaintance. If, at any time, you would like to volunteer for our program, please don't hesitate to contact me," Crystal said as she handed her a business card.

"Well, I do have two little ones at home. And, I'm so pleased to say that just this morning I found out that I'm pregnant again. But, I'm certain that I'll be able to help out at some time in the future. It's such an important cause," Ellen said sincerely.

"Congratulations on the news about the baby. Your husband must be thrilled," Crystal said as she shook Ellen's hand perfunctorily.

"Oh, I haven't told Darius yet, but I will tonight," Ellen said with a twinkle in her eye.

CHAPTER 7

MITCH WAS HEADING for a meeting with Mary Jo and Darius Davis. He had had a difficult time finding the quaint little restaurant hidden behind a large shopping center. Even though he lived in the area since he was a boy, he seldom went out to eat, so he was totally unfamiliar with places like *Hideaway Haven.*

He tried to picture in his mind what this Darius fellow would look like. Maybe a bit like his own brother, who was a big CEO for a financial firm in Singapore. He assumed that Davis would probably be wearing a suit and tie with cuff links peeking out from under his sleeves. In other words, a stuffed shirt. And, here he was in his usual flannel shirt and jeans, now wondering if his choice of clothing today had been a big mistake. He had enough self-pride that he didn't want the president of a firm classifying him as some *hick from the sticks.* That term was one of his brother's favorites, especially when he would catch Mitch standing up in the kitchen eating his breakfast. Why that annoyed his brother so much was something Mitch was never able to figure out.

Mitch finally found the inn and pulled into a parking spot alongside the steps leading to a long wide porch that wrapped around the restaurant. A Douglas fir, covered with small white lights, stood to the right of the doorway. More decorations, along with a fireplace where several logs were crackling, brought the small restaurant to life. He spotted Mary Jo seated at a table with a guy in a shirt that was opened at the neck. He laughed to himself because he didn't look a thing like his hoity-toity brother.

As soon as he approached the table, Darius stood up and stretched out his well-manicured hand. "Welcome, Mitch. I'm so glad that you decided to join us in our charity gala. I'm Darius Davis, President of Davis Media."

"I can thank Mary Jo for suggesting the idea to me," Mitch said as he sat down across from the two of them.

"I shared some information with Darius about your sanctuary, but I would appreciate your telling him just how it got started and what your mission is," Mary Jo said sweetly.

Mitch took off his jacket and leaned back in his chair. He didn't fail to notice that Mary Jo and Darius were sitting rather close together. "Well, let's see, after college and a stint in the army, I decided to come back home. I've been to many places, but love it here in Riverton. Just a few years ago, I inherited my parent's farm. Well, it was left to my brother and me, but he wanted no part of it, so I bought him out. I tried renting out the land to a local farmer but that didn't work out at all. I received offers from two industries who expressed interest in building plants there, but I didn't want to turn the land over to them. It's a beautiful spot. The land slopes down and comes to rest at the Timber Run River. My dad loved the land. In his Irish brogue, he used to say that the land was everything. 'They don't call it real estate for nothing' he used to tell us," Mitch paused, smiled and then said, "Am I being too wordy?"

"No," Darius said. "I really want to hear about your sanctuary."

"My mom loved animals. She especially loved those that were injured, deformed, or in need of special care. When we were kids, my mom and dad entered the St. Patrick's Day parade. Dad built an ark with hand-carved shamrocks down the sides. Then they put some of mom's cast-off animals on it. It was the hit of the parade.

29

I used to go down to the river every day in case any ducklings got separated from their mothers. Mom would say that the river coughed them up so that we could take care of them. So, I naturally followed in her footsteps—*Eliza's Animal Sanctuary* was named after her. All of the animals have special needs and will live out their lives on the farm. They are not very adoptable; however, every once in a while, someone falls in love with one of these poor animals and adopts him. Like Walter."

It started gradually. Someone would drop off a dog or cat and it would find its way to my back porch. Or, I would hear about a handicapped farm animal that was going to be put down. These animals are like potato chips—I couldn't stop. Anyway, there always seemed to be room for one more. And, you know, they seem to know that they have a *forever home* and are out of danger. They actually seem to be grateful."

However, it is expensive. I have a small allotment coming in each month. And, every month someone deposits money in my account. I can't be certain, but I think it's from my brother. We don't get along very well, but I sure do appreciate the money. So, I kind of live from pay check to pay check. But, I can't see myself doing anything else."

"Mitch, running a place like that takes work. Do you have any employees?" Darius asked.

"Not paid ones. I have two ladies from town who volunteer and they show up at least three to four days a week. Then there's Dave. He's a disabled farmer who had to sell his farm and is there every day. He's my right arm," Mitch said.

"I appreciate hearing about your animals," Darius said in a tone that revealed true interest. "What does your animal family include?"

"Well, right now, besides the cats and dogs, I have some goats, three horses, a pot-bellied pig, a peacock, a llama, dozens of ducks and chickens, and oh, even an albino owl that can't fly," Mitch said proudly. "And, each animal has a name. By the way, Mary Jo, my staff gave Walter his name. How's he doing?"

"Otto couldn't be happier. Walter and he are now joined at the hip. They love one another," Mary Jo replied.

"You know, using an ark and filling it with animals, is a great idea for the STAIRS event. Perhaps we could get a permit from the town council to put it in the center of Riverton Park," Darius suggested. "We also need to get something published on the abuse of animals. You know, something that people will take away as a reminder of the vital needs of these animals. Mary Jo told me what happened to Walter and I'm glad that they chased those dog fighters out of the area. They were disgusting."

"I have another idea. Since each animal has a name, let's start an adoption program. People can choose an animal that they want to help support financially. They could go to the sanctuary for visits to see how their adopted pet is getting along. In some cases, an animal could actually leave the sanctuary. But when that's not possible—let's say if the animal is too needy, or it's not possible for the adopter to house their pet—they'll still have the opportunity to interact. Each animal could have multiple adopters. What do you two think?" Mary Jo asked excitedly.

Darius suddenly put his arms around Mary Jo and hugged her. "Mary Jo, you're not only beautiful, but you're a genius."

Mitch was taken back. He suddenly felt like an outsider. And, to his complete surprise, he felt a pang of jealousy. Before they ended their meeting, Mary Jo reminded Mitch about the STAIRS meeting the following week.

As he got into his truck, he turned to watch Mary Jo and Darius get into a car. He called out "See you at the next meeting," but doubted that they even heard him.

CHAPTER 8

MARY JO HAD just finished writing up the monthly report and was pleased when she read over the figures. Twelve dogs had been adopted out in November and the donations had increased by four percent. She fully expected December's totals to be even higher since there were usually more adoptions during the holiday season. When the door opened and she spied her friend Cindy, she was surprised.

Quickly closing her laptop and running around the counter, she said excitedly, "Cindy, what a nice surprise! I haven't seen you in a while," Mary Jo said as she hugged her friend tightly.

"Well, you know what they say about the mountain not coming to you, so I decided I'd go to the mountain," Cindy said with a smile.

"What on earth does that mean? Cindy, I've just been so busy lately," Mary Jo replied, trying to hide the guilt that she felt.

"I want to become a volunteer. That way, I can do something good for the community, but more importantly, I'll get to see you more often," Cindy said as she pulled her hoody off.

Mary Jo just shook her head. "We'll be pleased to have you join us. With Maggie in the hospital, we're short-handed around here."

"Maggie—you mean Maggie Adams, your boss? What happened?"

"She's having a knee replacement. While one of the women from headquarters will take over for her, she only will be here on a part-time basis—you know, to make decisions and to sign documents, and things like that," Mary Jo explained.

"So, if I start volunteering right now, you'll be my boss? I don't know if I'll be able to handle *that*," Cindy teased.

"Otto will be here shortly to start walking some of the dogs. But, meanwhile, I have two pit bulls that I walk myself since they have not taken the temperment test for placement yet. If you come with me, I'll show you how to handle them," Mary Jo said as she began to lead Cindy to the kennels."

"But I don't like pit bulls," Cindy replied, stopping in her tracks.

"Cindy, I know you don't. I was kidding. How about walking Cooper and Zoey...one is a Doodle and the other is a Golden Retriever? They're pals and easy to handle."

"Okay. Just so they're not pit bulls."

As they headed to the kennels, Cindy spied a man walking towards them. "I think you have a customer," she said to Mary Jo.

"Oh...oh...that's Darius Davis, our corporate sponsor for STAIRS," Mary Jo said nervously. As Darius approached, Mary Jo put her hand out and said, "Hello, Darius. I want you to meet my dear friend Cindy Grove. Cindy, this is Darius Davis, President of Davis Media."

"Nice to meet you, Cindy. Mary Jo, I don't mean to interrupt your busy day, but I just wanted you to know that David Rutter has agreed to have his dogs perform for one of your events at the symposium. Cindy, are you familiar with David's Dancing Dogs?"

"Is he the one who won first place in the Animals on Parade Show recently?" she asked.

"Yes. One of his cousins works for me as a designer. Due to his tight schedule, Rutter said he only can donate two shows for your cause during the first week of June. Isn't that fantastic? I think we'll have sold out signs for both of those. He recommends that we use the arena at the farm show building since that will hold more people and it will also provide an ideal venue for his dogs," Darius said, obviously pleased with his accomplishment. "And, with your permission, I'll make the arrangements with Elliott Schmidt at the farm show to reserve the space."

Mary Jo had to restrain herself. She wanted to throw her arms around Darius but caught herself in time. She reached for his hand to shake it, when Darius grabbed her instead and said, "Excuse me, Mary Jo, but I'm so excited about this...but I guess you can tell that. Well, I've got to run. I'll see you at the next STAIRS meeting," he called over his shoulder as he waved and ran down the walkway.

Mary Jo was trying desperately to remain calm. "He's a great corporate sponsor," she said, trying to conceal her excitement. "In case all of this sounds confusing, each charity is expected to conduct activities that will get people directly involved in their cause. For instance, the YWCA is planning to hold amateur painting class, a swimming competition, and several other events. The idea is that if we get our donors in our buildings, or help them to learn more about our causes, they'll develop a sense of ownership."

Just then Mitch came in the door carrying a kitten in his arms. "I know you already have quite a few of these little guys, but someone dropped Samson off at my place. He looks as if he is in perfect health, so I thought someone might want to adopt him for Christmas," Mitch said as he handed the kitten to Mary Jo.

"Oh, he's precious. Mitch, this is Cindy Grove, a dear friend of mine."

As Cindy shook hands with Mitch, she said, "You know, my husband just mentioned your place the other day. He was wondering if the public is allowed to visit."

"You bet. We love to have visitors. Tell him that the best time to see all the different animals is any time after one o'clock. By that time they are usually all cleaned up and ready to show themselves off," Mitch said as he smiled broadly. He reached into his jacket pocket and pulled out a brochure. "Take this along, Cindy. It provides directions to our little farm. I'm on my way to check out another handicapped horse, so I better get moving." As he went out the door, he turned and said, "Mary Jo, I'll see you at the next meeting."

"Thanks for Samson," Mary Jo said.

"Wow, Mary Jo, do you always get such good-looking men here?" Cindy asked. "One dark and handsome, and one with shoulders that won't quit."

"Our goal here, my charming friend, is to find homes for our animals," Mary Jo replied as she blushed.

"Well, that's a great idea. Now, are you going to put me to work or not?" Cindy asked playfully.

"Okay, sweetie. The second week of each month, we take two dogs to the nursing home. There we meet in the activity room where residents are waiting to meet our dogs. We walk them around and allow residents to pet them and fuss over them. The dogs love it. But, more importantly, you can see the expressions on the residents' faces as they interact with the dogs," Mary Jo explained.

"Do the dogs wear muzzles?" Cindy asked.

"Oh, no. The dogs must be approved by our vet before they are allowed to participate in this activity. He puts them through tests to make certain that they are friendly and people-oriented. Then, on the fourth week of the month, we do the same thing with kittens."

"Count me out on that," Cindy said firmly. "No cats for me."

"No pit bulls, no cats...how about snakes?"

"Now I *know* you're kidding. You surely don't take snakes to a nursing home," Cindy insisted.

Mary Jo laughed. "You're right. Now, let's take you to meet the rest of the team."

"This sounds like fun," Cindy said. "By the way, if I had to choose between your two male visitors, I would pick the one with those broad shoulders. He has an honest face and a genuine smile that lights up a whole room."

CHAPTER 9

J OSHUA FADDEN WAS extremely uncomfortable. He had regretted accepting the invitation to this *Guys' Night Out* to celebrate his old friend's upcoming wedding, but he had felt that he was obligated. The dinner was tedious—a little too raucous for his taste. Now, here he was, in his expensive tailored suit and imported silk tie with its perfect Windsor knot, jammed into a smoke-filled, dirty-looking room with men who apparently couldn't get enough of looking at naked women. He wasn't used to being in a strip club, and he felt very awkward pretending that he was having a good time. His wife, Crystal, surprisingly had encouraged him to go by reminding him that his friend's father was a very important member of the Woodward Country Club. He tried to become invisible by hanging back as the rest of the party group acted like asses as they stuffed money into each stripper's G-string.

"Come on, Phil, sit over here. We have a surprise for you," one of the guys called out to the honoree. Phil, who was feeling no pain, rushed over just as the stripper jumped off the stage and headed for her next lap dance.

Joshua moved as far away from the stripper as he could without being too obvious. She certainly wasn't very attractive, but she was wowing the crowd by letting her huge breasts bounce back and forth. The music was extremely loud and the crowd was screaming for more and more action. When the stripper pushed her breasts into Phil's face, Joshua couldn't stand it any longer. He worked his way to the side door and disappeared, never noticing that a short, stocky man was right behind him. Joshua figured that Phil was so intoxicated that he wouldn't miss him at all.

As Joshua got into his BMW, he wasn't aware that someone was taking pictures of him with a cell phone. When he drove out of the parking lot, he breathed a sigh of relief. Now, he still had time to stop by Morgan's apartment with that little pre-Christmas present. Proud that he had been able to keep his relationship with Morgan a secret from everyone, he felt exhilarated. Morgan would know exactly what to do to wipe away the things that he had been exposed to in that seedy strip club. It wouldn't be long until he would be running Fadden Insurance with Morgan waiting for him at home. Meanwhile, the little rotund man followed at a safe distance.

Two hours later, when Joshua stepped out of the doorway and turned to kiss Morgan goodnight, his stalker almost dropped his cell phone when he realized that Joshua was kissing another man. "Bingo!" Henry said excitedly. He chuckled—what a great Christmas present for me.

CHAPTER 10

G REG HAD AN appointment with Sarah Hamilton McIntyre, one of the wealthiest women in the Commonwealth. He had been trying to get her attention for many months, when, out of the blue, she had called him. He immediately did extensive research on the families. He discovered that the Hamiltons had made their money by manufacturing the equipment needed by the saw mills and the furniture-making factories. When old man Hamilton died, his two daughters sold the business for a record-breaking amount of money.

He knew where Hamilton mansion was located, but he never before had driven through those very impressive iron gates emblazoned with gold letters that announced Hamilton Haven. The entrance way was beautifully decorated for Christmas. Red satin bows, attached to every lamp post, were waving gently in the early December breeze.

Greg was wearing his newest tailor-made suit and he was clean shaven. The extensive research that he had done on this client provided him with the kind of information that he could use to make an excellent first impression. Mrs. McIntyre did not like facial hair, so he had said goodbye to his mustache. He carried a small bouquet of violets arranged neatly in a little cut glass vase. He rang the doorbell and cleared his throat. He was pleasantly surprised when the door opened to see a rather young-looking, tall, and thin ninety-two-year old widow standing in the doorway.

"Good morning, Mrs. McIntyre. I'm Greg Fadden. These are for you," he said courteously as he handed her the bouquet.

"Oh, violets. They're my favorite. Where on earth did you find them at this time of year?" she asked as she opened the door wide.

"My florist gets the credit for knowing where to find them," Greg responded.

"Come in. Please have a seat. I'll be right back. I want to take care of these lovely violets," Sarah said as she hurried away.

Greg took advantage of her departure by examining the elegant well-appointed living room. Huge poinsettia plants seemed to be everywhere. The staircase leading to the second floor was festooned with fresh garland and pine cones. Beyer figurines had been placed in small groups on the side tables. The room was breath-taking. On one side of the room stood a Steinway grand piano. He strolled over to take a look at the sheet music that was there—Debussy's *Clair de Lune*. The piano bench was a bit askew, as if she had been playing before he had arrived. Greg was not a music aficionado, so when he read about Sarah's love of Debussy's work, he had listened to several recordings and read a book about the musician's life.

"I see you found it—my other true love," Sarah said as she lovingly placed her hands on the Steinway. "I used to play fairly well, but lately...well... my fingers no long cooperate very well," Sarah said as she smiled.

"Debussy," Greg said as he pointed to the sheet music. "He revolutionized piano playing. He's given credit for absorbing music from all kinds of cultures and creating French music that invokes pastel flowers and beautiful women."

"It's so nice to know that there are those who understand great music," Sarah said as she took a seat alongside Greg. "I guess you know that Debussy got his inspiration for *Clair de Lune* from a poem written by Verlaine about victorious love. You see, I'm an old fool—still reminiscing about love."

"Your home is exquisite," Greg said. "The decorations are perfect and everything is done in such good taste."

"Thank you. I asked you to come today since a friend of mine, Estelle Ford, told me about your foundation and I think it may be the answer to my problem. You see, I have recently inherited money from my sister's estate. I don't want to add that to my investments. Heaven knows, I don't need to worry about making more money. At the same time, since I have no family left anymore, I would like to do something to, you know, I think they say "pay it forward" now-a-days. I looked over the informational pieces you sent me, but I wanted to talk with you personally since this is a rather large amount."

"I'm privileged to have this opportunity, Mrs. McIntyre. Mrs. Ford is a charming lady and a wise investor," Greg said excitedly. The time he had spent researching the family was time well spent. Sarah was beginning to treat him like a trusted advisor.

"I understand that your foundation has provided hundreds of needy souls with funds for education, medical treatments, and housing. Is this correct?"

"Mrs. McIntyre, we have a plan for clients like you. First, let me say that we take our job as your fiduciary agent seriously and will put your interests first at all times. I can provide you with printouts of all the wonderful things that the Fadden Foundation has done. While we cannot give you names and addresses, I can take you around the county and point out some of the miraculous things that we have done with funds from clients who were in a similar situation," Greg said as he inched a bit closer to Sarah.

"I don't think that's necessary. Estelle told me such uplifting tales about your foundation that I'll take her word for it. I also plan to turn over my precious Hamilton Haven to the foundation. I'm certain that Grandfather Hamilton would approve. However, I have one stipulation to which the Fadden Foundation must agree."

"And that is?"

"My Steinway. That must go to the Riverton School of Music. I want you to invest this check wisely so that it grows much larger by the time they receive my piano," she said as she placed the check in front of Greg, who had to keep his reaction under control when he got a look at the seven-figure check. "When I'm gone, you'll be free to do whatever you need to do with the rest of my estate. Now what must we do to make this legal?" Sarah asked.

"We'll set up a meeting with your investment agent and our legal representative and, in no time at all, the paperwork will be done. May we recognize you in our brochure?"

"No. I don't want that. Once I'm gone from this earth, and I join my dear husband, there is no need for anyone to know what I did with my possessions. Please, no recognition. I think that is so self-serving," Sarah demurred.

"I know. I have a splendid idea. What about scholarships? When your investment funds move into your Trust account, we could award scholarships to students who want to pursue a degree in music. I'm certain that these grateful students will be honored, knowing who made their dreams come true, and they will be proud to represent you as they work to develop their musical talent. Your love of good music will infuse itself into who-knows-how-many generations."

"That's a wonderful idea," Sarah said. "Oh, let's include giving grants to schools for their music programs. I don't have to be a lonely old lady, pining away in gloom and doom. Life has been good to me. I have been given so much—way too much. Greg, thank you for opening my eyes. Now I have something to look forward to. I'm so glad Estelle told me about you. I know I can trust you."

"We **will** follow all your directions, Mrs. McIntyre. Now, I have a favor to ask you."

"Ask away," Sarah said as she patted Greg's hand.

"Will you please play your piano for me? I love Debussy. It would be an honor for me to hear his music again," Greg said as he pointed to the Steinway.

"Before I start playing," Sarah said coyly, "I have something to tell you. You see, you very well could have been my nephew. I once had a crush on your Uncle Roger. I was twenty-five and Roger was only eighteen and when Grandfather Hamilton became aware of my little fascination with Roger, he quickly sent me to Aunt Francine in the Hamptons. Good thing he did, though, because I met Humphrey McIntyre, a ruggedly handsome and wealthy young man," she giggled. "I quickly forgot all about Roger," she said quite bashfully.

"I would have loved to have been your nephew, but it was Uncle Roger who missed out on a beautiful gem."

Sarah and Greg sat side by side on the piano bench, while Sarah allowed the understated melancholic heart of Claude Debussy's music to fill her living room one more time.

Greg thought it ironic that he had come so close to becoming related to Sarah. However, the way things were turning out, he might be able to make Hamilton Haven the site of Fadden Foundation. And, that would mean he could drive through those gates every day. He also thanked his lucky stars that Sarah's crush was foiled by the very wealthy Humphrey McIntyre, who had apparently swept Sarah off her feet. Now, remarkably, Hamilton Haven would soon be under his control. He could add another trophy to those he had already amassed. But, this would be the richest one of all.

As he drove out the driveway, Greg took a second look at the decorations. It was important to him to memorize exactly how it appeared. When he was in charge of this estate, he wanted it to look as enchanting as it did now. As he reviewed what happened today, he suddenly realized that while Roger missed capturing Sarah, all her money would be coming into the Fadden coffers. Sweet!

CHAPTER 11

H ENRY HENDERSON WAS out of breath as he climbed the stairs that led to his little office on the second floor. This morning, when he woke up, he really wanted to just roll over and catch a few more winks; but then, he remembered that he had lots of planning to get the most money out of what he had learned about Joshua Fadden. Since Roger was willing to pay to have four different people tailed, and if his good luck continued, he could shake down more than just one person—maybe all of them. The first bit of good luck had been spotting one of Fadden's nephews kissing a man. While most people wouldn't really care about such a relationship, Roger Fadden would probably go ballistic. And, Henry was betting that Joshua would not be too eager to have his lover dragged through the mud.

Henry pulled out his electric immersion heater from his top desk drawer and plunked it into a nasty-looking, chipped cup. He tossed in some Sanka and held the cup under the water faucet. While he waited for the brew to get hot, he began printing out all the pictures he had taken with his phone—those that he took inside the strip club, and the winning photo that showed Joshua and some man locking lips. He also eagerly printed out a photo of the stripper as she was sitting on some guy's lap and tucked that in his wallet.

45

He chuckled when he realized that he had chosen Joshua first because he had thought the man would be easy to eliminate since he had such a squeaky-clean reputation. Now, Henry needed to play his cards right. He could blackmail Joshua and hold off reporting anything to Fadden about his younger nephew just to let the money flow into his pockets.

Until recently, Henry had been content to take small cases, but the rewards had been meager. He needed more jobs like the one Roger had given him a few months ago. All he had had to do was deliver a duffel bag to some guy in Pittsburgh. He had been instructed to use the bus and, as long as he didn't disturb the contents of the bag, he would get five thousand dollars. He had done what he was told and Roger was true to his word.

Now, however, the thought of blackmail excited him. He must make his plans carefully. What if Joshua refused to pay? While he took a few sips of his coffee, he began to work on a solution if this happened. Hell, the guy had a wife with expensive tastes—inheriting his uncle's fortune could ease the pain. And, in order to be an heir, Joshua needed to keep his uncle happy. Perhaps he needed to meet his target in a public place—where he could not put up a fuss. He pulled out the notes he had created on Joshua and discovered that the perp usually went to the gym two times a week. So, Henry planned to be in the locker room and he'd greet Joshua with a copy of the damning photo. Out loud, Henry said, "Surprise, Lover Boy!"

Henry was extremely pleased with himself. He was brilliant. One by one he would be able to blackmail the nephews and their wives and still get a payoff from Roger. He didn't have to have Santa bring him a present—he would create his own.

CHAPTER 12

T HE HOUSE WAS very quiet. Mary Jo was aimlessly staring out the window. She wasn't certain why she hadn't moved from that spot. She assumed it was guilt that was overpowering her. While no one knew about Darius yet—the operative word was yet—if this affair continued, they would. Suppose that's all there will be—an affair. That thought frightened her so badly that she felt a tear running down her cheek. If it's just an affair, then no one else needed to know what happened. But that's not what she really wanted. She wanted Darius.

Greg would be home late this evening, and she wasn't looking forward to his presence. As she turned around, Mary Jo felt as if she were imprisoned. She had created her own incarceration. She began to wonder what life would be like if she and Darius were a couple. Beth was the one that she worried about the most. Greg would probably just accept the situation and move on with his career. Uncle Roger would never forgive her, and he could very well take out his resentment on Greg. And then there were the children—Darius's. *I must not think about them now. I just can't.*

If her parents were alive, they would be mortified. No one in the family had ever gotten a divorce. Well, that was then; this was now. Their little assignations had happened six or seven times by now. It was time to confront Darius with her concerns: He needed to let her know if they were just friends with benefits, or were they going to stand up against the world and become a couple? Her mind was racing. She was jolted back to the present when the doorbell rang. Peering through the little peephole, she saw Cindy standing there with a gift bag in her hand. Heaving an unrepressed sigh, Mary Jo opened the door slowly.

"Oh," Cindy said excitedly, "you're home. I was hoping you would go with me to the opening of the new art center."

Trying to smile, Mary Jo replied, "I've been so busy with this charity thing that I forgot all about that."

"Here," Cindy said, as she handed the gift bag to her friend, "I picked up a pack of brownies from that new bakery downtown. I thought we could enjoy them over a cup of coffee and then we could go to the opening. What do you say?"

"Great idea," Mary Jo said as she headed to the kitchen with Cindy following behind.

After some small talk about Cindy's experiences volunteering at the shelter, the two were finally seated side by side, simultaneously stirring their coffee. Cindy leaned back in her chair and said, "Look, I don't know how to begin this conversation, but here I go. Mary Jo, what in the hell s going on? I have sensed that something is... not right. You never look directly at me anymore. Have I done something wrong? Would you rather I didn't come to the shelter to help?"

Mary Jo bit her lip. After a few seconds of deafening silence, she took a deep breath and said, "You've done nothing wrong. And, I love having you at the shelter. What I need right now is a friend to share my burden."

"My God," Cindy said a bit annoyed, "since when have I not been a friend, Mary Jo? You know that you can share anything with me. If you don't know that by now, all these past years have been in vain."

"You may not want to be my friend any longer."

"Don't be ridiculous," Cindy said as she put her mug down on the table.

Avoiding Cindy's eyes, Mary Jo said, "I'm having an affair."

Cindy's mouth opened wide but nothing came out. She finally blurted out, "What? Seeing another man? You? Does Greg know?"

"No."

"May I ask—who? No, wait...it's that Darius fellow, isn't it?"

Mary Jo began pacing. "I know it's wrong. I've known that from the start. But, Cindy, I'm in love with him. Please, please, don't hate me."

"I could never hate you. But, Mary Jo, what about his wife and children?"

"Darius told me that he and his wife have been living separate lives for a long time. They have an arrangement that when the youngest child begins school, they'll separate. It seems that she wants to go back to college to finish her degree. He said that the children will spend equal time with both of them," Mary Jo said as her voice became weaker and weaker.

"Honey, are you ready to care for little ones?" Cindy asked. "Wait a minute—how old is this guy? It sounds like his wife might be lots younger than he is."

"Darius is our age. His current wife was only nineteen when they married."

Cindy couldn't believe her ears. "How did he get mixed up with someone so young?"

"Well, she had been hired to help take care of Darius's mother. She was like a companion. She would make her lunch, read to her and keep her company," Mary Jo tried to explain.

However, she didn't fail to take notice that Cindy didn't like her answer.

Cindy wanted to remind Mary Jo that Darius had robbed the cradle when he got involved with the companion. How was she going to help her friend who had been blinded by this guy? "When do you plan on telling Greg?"

"Not for a while. If I can keep this from him for at least a year, it would be better all around," Mary Jo explained.

"It sounds as if you've already made up your mind. You really don't need any advice from me," Cindy said softly.

"I'm sorry that it sounds that way. I've been unhappy for so many years that now that I have found Darius, I know what happiness is. My parents felt that, when you got married, you were married for life. I don't accept that premise. His children are young; they'll come around. Greg, well…he'll probably not even bat an eyelash. Beth is the one I'm worried about," Mary Jo said as she sat down again.

"How do you think Uncle Roger will take all of this?" Cindy asked.

"First, he'll condemn me to Hell. But he'll probably be glad in the long run when I'm out of the family."

Suddenly, Mary Jo fell to her knees in front of Cindy. She lifted her head, and with tears streaming down her face, she managed to say, "Don't abandon me, Cindy. I need you now more than ever. I can't help it. I love Darius with every fiber of my being. I can't imagine giving him up."

The two of them sat that way for a few minutes; Mary Jo with her face in Cindy's lap while Cindy stroked Mary Jo's hair.

"I will always be here for you—no matter what you decide," Cindy said with compassion. "I wish I were wise enough to give you the words you need to hear at this moment. However, when we violate trust, we must realize that there is a cost to pay. You need to think this through. Just remember, Mary Jo, once you make your decision, you must find a way to live not only with that choice but to live with yourself."

Mary Jo wiped her eyes. "When our relationship turned physical, I can't say that I was surprised. While I didn't start out thinking that I was going to commit adultery, I allowed it to happen. Cindy, Darius and I are deeply in love."

"Are you certain that he's as committed as you are?"

Mary Jo didn't respond immediately. Slowly, she looked up at Cindy and asked, "Why?"

"Sweetie, if he can cheat on his wife with you, what makes you think he won't cheat on you with someone else?"

CHAPTER 13

I T WAS FRIDAY morning and Mary Jo was in the kitchen preparing Greg's breakfast. She tried not to think about last night. How she had ever gotten through it, she would never know. When Greg rolled over last night and touched her, she shivered. Greg noticed her reaction. She explained it away as a chill because she might be coming down with a cold. While Greg's lovemaking was always brief without any foreplay, it was worse than ever. She tried to block out all thoughts of Darius, but she was not successful, so she did what Aunt Emma had told her to do—she shut her eyes. It was over quickly.

As Greg started eating his eggs and bacon, he said, "Mary Jo, I've got to leave on Monday morning. The requests we've been getting for our new investment plan are piling up and I'd rather not ask Joshua for help—it's just not his forte. So, how about we go out for dinner tonight?"

"Okay. Just make reservations anywhere. What's on your schedule today?" Mary Jo asked.

"I've an appointment with Roger and then I'm free if you have something in mind," Greg said as he sipped his coffee.

"No. I'm going to refill the bird feeders, and then I have some shopping to do," Mary Jo said as she began stacking the dishes in the washer.

"Okay. I really need to do some more paperwork in order to be ready for my next consultations," Greg said as he kissed her on the cheek and walked away.

Mary Jo got the bird feed out of the garage and headed to the front yard. While Greg had hired a landscaper to do most of the work, Mary Jo wanted to take care of her feeders herself. Just as she knelt down, she heard a voice behind her.

"Hello, Mrs. Fadden," Otto said as he guided Walter up the walkway.

"Hello, Otto, and, of course, Walter. Both of you look splendid. You sure take good care of him," Mary Jo said as she hugged Walter.

"He was groomed yesterday," Otto said proudly. "My friend, Roger, is so good to us. He takes care of everything."

"Walter, you are one lucky dog," Mary Jo remarked, as she patted his head.

"Walter is a good dog. I taught him not to go into the kitchen. Roger doesn't want any dogs in his kitchen. Walter will sit right outside the kitchen door, but he never goes in. He's a good dog. Mary Jo, do you have any dead Indians buried in your yard?"

Mary Jo almost dropped the bag of bird feed. "What? Dead Indians?"

"Roger has some under his roses. Walter's not supposed to go near them. You see they died when they attacked a covered wagon," Otto explained. "He gives me historical lessons," Otto explained.

"Oh, history lessons. I see," Mary Jo smiled. She didn't know that Roger could actually be humorous at all. "You two make a good pair," Mary Jo said as she hugged Walter.

"Well, we better get going. We must pick up some things at the store for dinner tonight. Come on, Walter, we have work to do," Otto directed. "We're having my favorite tonight—hot dogs."

Mary Jo smiled as she watched Otto and Walter walk away. She never understood why Roger made friends with Otto, but she was pleased that he had. Otto stopped by Mary Jo's frequently, so she was able to check on Walter. There probably was no other dog in the state that was loved as much as Otto loved Walter.

As she thought about this, Greg came out the front door. "Roger just called and wants to see me earlier, so I'll see you later. By the way, we have reservations at Greenfield Manor for dinner at 6:30. See you later," Greg said over his shoulder as he got into his car and pulled away. Mary Jo was speechless. Greenfield Manor was where she had had lunch with Darius just a few days ago.

All afternoon, Mary tried to think of a way that she could get Greg to go anywhere else for dinner besides Greenfield Manor. She would have to sit across the table from her husband, while memories of Darius would be floating in and out of her mind. Perhaps, if she could get Cindy and her husband to go along, it would be easier to carry on a light conversation. Then, again, perhaps Russ wasn't even home. To get her mind moving in another direction, she starting going through her clothes to choose something to wear—certainly not that sexy-looking number that she had worn for Darius. Maybe she could tell Greg that she wasn't feeling well. A hat—that's it—she would wear the floppy hat that almost hid her face.

By the time Greg arrived home, Mary Jo had showered and dressed. She had already placed her purse and hat on the chair by the front door. "How was Roger?" she asked, as Greg came through the door.

"I'm concerned. He didn't seem himself today. He just doesn't look well," Greg responded. "He did, though, congratulate me on my latest foundation account sale."

"You better get moving, Greg. Greenfield Manor doesn't hold

reservations too long on a Friday night," Mary Jo said, trying to sound casual.

As they drove to the restaurant, Greg said, "You look great in that hat."

Mary Jo almost fainted. Greg was certainly not known for his compliments.

"Thank you," Mary Jo replied. "Oh, I have something funny to tell you. While I was filling the bird feeders, Otto stopped by. He asked me if I knew that there were dead Indians buried in Roger's garden."

Greg chuckled. "What?"

"Yeah, dead Indians. I believe that Roger was trying to teach Otto some history lessons so he might have made up little stories to help him understand. At least that's what I was finally able to gather from our little conversation," Mary Jo said as she adjusted the brim of her hat.

"I don't know how Otto ever talked Roger into allowing him to get a dog, but he did. It seems that Otto and his dog are joined at the hip. I've got to give accolades to Roger for not only taking care of Otto, but also putting up with a damned dog," Greg said as he escorted Mary Jo into the restaurant.

"I thought you liked dogs. You're beginning to sound like Crystal," Mary Jo remarked, obviously disturbed by what her husband had said. Mary Jo was relieved when they were seated in a small alcove that was on the other side of the room from where she had been with Darius. She kept telling herself that all would be well and this evening wouldn't last forever.

"I need to share some information with you about the company. Roger is making some managerial changes. I thought that you might like to know what his plans are."

Mary Jo was surprised. Greg seldom talked about the company. "Isn't this a bit unusual?"

Greg hadn't missed Mary Jo's sharp comment. He bit his lip and leaned back in his chair. "Mary Jo, please. This isn't the time nor place to begin one of your drawn-out arguments. Do you want to know what happened today, or not?"

Mary Jo sighed. "Of course, I do."

"Roger's made some changes permanent. Joshua is now fully in charge of both the insurance and the real estate divisions. I'll head the investment division and the Fadden Foundation. I know Joshua is pleased, since he has really been doing most of the work in these areas for some time now. And, since I'm the one who's responsible for making our investment division so successful, I certainly wanted to be formally in charge. In addition, I have great ideas for the Fadden Foundation, and now I don't have to request permission from Roger to do anything."

"Well, then, congratulations. We can think of tonight as a celebration," Mary Jo suggested.

"However, Roger is acting very much like a man who knows that the end is near," Greg cautioned.

"You don't mean…" Mary Jo appeared shocked.

"He didn't give me any particulars. However, I did think he looked a bit more fragile than he has been in the past," Greg replied. "Nonetheless, I think he made excellent decisions. Joshua will do extremely well with his assignment. I love to work with investments, and I have always found running the Foundation exciting. You're going to like this part—he's made plans for Beth as well," Greg said proudly.

"Greg, are you sure that she'll want to go along with **his** plans? She may very well want to make her own way. It may be that she will get married before too long," Mary Jo said less than enthusiastically.

"Did she tell you that she's serious about anyone?" Greg questioned.

"Well, no, but you can never tell. I really don't want her getting married so young," Mary Jo added.

"We married young," Greg said, looking for a reaction.

Mary Jo had to look away. She had never told Greg that she had tried to back out of their wedding, but even now, she could not be that cruel. He would learn soon enough.

"I just want Beth to try her wings a bit before she considers marriage. After all, she should be able to choose her own path as far as her career is concerned, and I think she could do that very well without Roger's interference," Mary Jo said curtly.

"I know that. But, she'll, at least, have the opportunity to go in that direction if she chooses. Don't let your dislike of Roger get in the way," Greg said not trying to hide his annoyance.

All was quiet between them for some time. Mary Jo nervously picked at the food on her plate, while Greg worked on his second glass of wine.

"Maybe this is not a good time to ask you a question, but here goes. I would like to know if you would agree to serve on The Fadden Foundation Board. I truly believe that the current makeup of the board sometimes lacks a woman's point of view," Greg said as convincingly as he could.

"Is Crystal going to be asked to serve, too?"

Greg laughed. "Heavens, no. What gave you that idea?"

"She won't be happy if I'm on the board and she isn't."

"I guess I'll have to live with her unhappiness," Greg said as he laid his credit card on the little silver tray.

"Let me think about that for a while, Greg,"

As the two of them headed for the front entrance, Mary Jo almost lost her composure when she spotted Darius escorting a woman back to the same little alcove that she and her husband had just vacated.

CHAPTER 14

HENRY WAS EXTREMELY nervous as he backed his car into a space behind the New Horizon Gym. He had to do this right or his whole plan would blow up in his face. Since this was the first time he had ever tried to blackmail someone, and he had no how-to book to follow, he had to depend on his gut instincts. He had timed Joshua's routine at the gym on Monday so he knew that the well-built man would take about an hour and ten minutes before he would enter the locker room to shower and change.

He went over the layout of the facility in his mind. Since he had been smart enough to case the place ahead of time, he knew that Joshua's locker was close to the rear emergency door. A long slated, highly polished, wooden bench ran down the center of the aisle. He decided that if the area became too crowded, he would approach Joshua in the parking lot.

As he walked by the registration desk, a muscular desk clerk looked up. "Back again, I see. Have you decided to join? We're running a special till the end of the month," he said as he revealed a set of perfectly straight, white teeth.

"Think I'll check around one more time. Maybe I'll be back. Oh, can I use a credit card?" Henry asked, feigning interest in membership.

"Sure thing," the clerk responded.

Henry cut the conversation off when he spotted Joshua heading to his locker. Henry roamed around, looking over the equipment, giving Joshua time to shower and dress. When Henry entered the locker room, Joshua was putting his suit coat on.

"Mr. Fadden?" Henry asked innocently.

"Yes," Joshua replied as he looked over at the out-of-shape Henry.

Henry made himself as tall as possible and held the photo in front of Joshua's face.

Joshua took a step backwards. His eyes widened and his lips tightened. He was speechless.

"Did I get your attention?" Henry asked, pleased with himself. "I have the photo up for sale. Now, would you like to buy it, or shall I ask Uncle Roger?"

"I think we should go outside," Joshua responded as he grabbed his briefcase and headed for the door.

Joshua stood beside his car, while a breathless Henry strained to catch up with him. "You know," he said, "there is nothing illegal about that."

"Oh, I know. But, we both realize that Uncle Roger would not approve. If he knew about your little friend, you'd find yourself on the outside of Fadden Insurance in a heartbeat," Henry said. "Now, are you ready to buy?"

"How much?"

"Five thousand."

"And how often will you be coming back for more, you bastard."

"Now, now, that's not nice. It's the holiday season. Tell you what. Five would make me happy right now, but ten will keep me away forever," Henry said, pleased with his strategy. "Friday morning, when you come to the gym, bring ten grand wrapped in Christmas paper and give it to me. Do we have a bargain?"

"Okay. But, so help me, if you tell Roger, you will not be around much longer," Joshua said as he grabbed the photo.

Henry watched Joshua drive away. He could not help but smile. He did it. He was going to have a handsome payday. Joshua was going to follow his instructions. Now, what Henry must do next was to get something on Joshua's stuck-up wife. Then, just like at the racetrack—a daily double. Look out, Society Snob, I'm coming after your painted-up face next.

CHAPTER 15

M ARY JO HAD been upset the whole weekend. All she could think about was that woman who had been holding on to Darius' arm and smiling up at him. She would have to face him today at the STAIRS meeting. One moment she felt angry; the next betrayed. Perhaps she should just be quiet and let him open the conversation today. Or, should she just blow him off? She probably had no right being angry. After all, she was only the *other woman*—one with just a loose commitment for many months ahead—supposedly. And, to top it off, Crystal's name was on the agenda—it was surely going to be difficult to get through the meeting today.

As she got out of her car, she saw Darius holding a conversation with Holly Stevens, the YWCA representative. As soon as Holly saw Mary Jo, she waved at her and motioned for her to join them.

"Darius was just telling me about getting David's Dancing Dogs to perform four shows for your organization at the charity gala. How marvelous! David won first place on the Animals on Parade Show," Holly said excitedly.

"That's right. He's agreed to put on four shows as part of our charity event. He'll send us a list of items that he'll need to accommodate his dogs," Darius said as he squeezed Mary Jo's hand.

"Four shows? I thought it was only two," Mary Jo questioned.

"Well, you can thank my sister. You may not know it, but she's a talent agent. She was in town over the weekend, and I happened to mention STAIRS and that I was working with you on planning an event with David and his dogs. When she told me that she now represents David and thought that she could get him to perform more than twice for us, I jumped on it right away. I was so happy that I even treated her to dinner at Greenfield Manor Friday night," Darius explained as he guided Mary Jo into the meeting room.

It was all Mary Jo could do to stop herself from throwing her arms around Darius and begging for forgiveness. She would never tell him—no need to let him know how insecure she was. Jealously was a new feeling for her; one that she would have to get under control.

Eager to get on to another topic, Mary Jo turned to Holly and said, "How are plans for charity week coming along for the YWCA?"

"So far we have three events planned. In one of our rooms, two local artists will be giving group painting lessons. Students will have their own easels and set of paints as they try to follow the artists' instructions. In another area, we'll be giving belly dancing lessons. Maria Cruz, a dance instructor from New York, will be giving lessons. Then, in the pool area, we'll have a diving contest," Holly reported proudly.

"Isn't Maria the dancer who made such a hit in the latest Martin Defoe movie?" Mary Jo asked as she gratefully noticed that her normal voice level had returned.

"She's the one. We're expecting all our sessions to be sold out early. I'm looking forward to hearing the progress reports from the others," Holly said as she hurried to her seat.

Darius guided Mary Jo out into the hallway. "Mary Jo, is something wrong?" he asked gently.

Mary Jo was flustered. "I had a difficult weekend. I must apologize if I seem a bit edgy."

"I have the afternoon free. Are we on?" Darius asked under his breath.

"We're on."

"I have an idea regarding how we can get more people involved with the animal shelter," Darius said as they took seats at the meeting table. "Each person who purchases a ticket for a hundred dollars and agrees to walk a dog for at least twenty minutes, will get one lottery ticket for an all-expense paid vacation for two to one of three different locations—Hawaii, Las Vegas, or Alaska. Swisher Travel Agency has agreed to donate these wonderful prizes."

"Wow, Darius, what would such a prize be worth?" Mary Jo said as she grabbed Darius' arm.

"I guess about ten thousand or so. Swisher's will be celebrating their twenty-fifth anniversary and, since he's also a dog-lover, he felt that he and his wife would get a kick out of such an event. Mary Jo, you'll have people lined up around the block to walk dogs," Darius laughed, as he nodded his head. "You better make certain that you have extra leashes because it's possible all the dogs will be going on lots of walks."

"When David's dogs are here, I would like to have Walter act as the host," Mary Jo said.

"Oh, and who is this Walter guy?" Darius asked pointedly.

Mary Jo smiled. "He's a friend of mine," she said sweetly. "He comes to visit me several times a week. And, he's Otto's adopted dog."

Darius leaned in close to Mary Jo. "Otto...Walter...I need to check these guys out."

They were interrupted when the chairman said, "Crystal Faddden, chair of our opening day ceremonies, has something she wants to share with the group. Crystal, the floor is yours."

"Those of us who are working on developing a program for opening day for STAIRS are pleased to report that the Governor will provide a welcoming address. And, the US Army Band has agreed to play for us. We also will have statewide cable coverage. Isn't all of this thrilling?" Crystal gushed. "And to add a bit of icing to the cake, Roger Fadden has agreed to provide the funding necessary for this opening event."

When the crowd stood up and applauded, Crystal couldn't have been more pleased. She was still excited when she exited the meeting and headed for her car. She failed to notice a man leaning on her Mercedes.

"Hello, Mrs. Fadden," Henry said softly. "Or, should I say Lilly?"

Crystal's eyes opened wide. Her knees began to shake. She hadn't heard that name for years. She scanned the man's face, but she had no idea who he was. But, obviously, he knew about her past. She clung to the side of her car door.

"Have your attention?" Henry asked as he smiled. "We need to negotiate, my dear. Yes, I know all about you. Do you want Uncle Roger to know, too?"

Crystal just stared at him. Others from the meeting were now heading for the parking lot and she didn't know what to do. She kept telling herself to remain calm...maybe this was some kind of joke.

"I have the documents. I have photos. You may have them all if you deliver ten thousand dollars on Friday at ten. I'll be parked in the lot behind First National Bank to make it handy for you to make your withdrawal. If you go to the cops—if you tell anyone, even your husband—I'll make sure the press gets the entire bundle. If you agree to my terms, just shake your head."

As Crystal looked at Henry and shook her head, she suddenly put on a smile and waved to Mary Jo and Darius. Henry didn't fail to notice that Mary Jo, the next one on his list, was walking beside a man who was holding on to her elbow. As the man opened the car door for her, Henry was delighted when he noticed that the man playfully slapped Mary Jo on her backside. Henry hurried to his car to follow Mary Jo. He felt invigorated. He knew that he was an expert at following people without being caught. Out loud, he said, "I'm like one smart person."

CHAPTER 16

WHEN HIS PRIVATE phone rang early in the morning, Henry realized that it could only be one person—Roger Fadden. Damn. Roger ordered him to meet him and bring along all the files that he had on the Fadden family. Henry had planned on visiting Mary Jo today and let her know that she needed to pay him or else. Now he would have to wait—and Henry was no good at waiting. He hurriedly dressed, grabbed his notebook and most of the files, and headed to a bench on Hemlock Street next to Timber Run River right across from Roger's office. The only good thing about the day was that it was unusually warm for the week before Christmas. But Henry felt sick in the stomach trying to guess what Roger was up to. However, Henry had been careful, and he held back a few of the photos and other documents that might just come in handy in the future. Roger didn't need to know everything.

He spied Roger, sitting on the bench with his legs stretched out as if he didn't have a care in the world as he played with the handle of a large shopping bag that sat on the ground in front of his feet. Henry flopped down beside Roger and tried to smile. He hoped that Roger couldn't hear how badly his stomach was growling.

"What's up, friend?" Henry said as his voice shook a bit.

"It's going to snow later on today," Roger said in a flat voice.

"Nah, it's too warm to snow," Henry replied.

Roger ignored the contradiction and said, "Did you ever really watch the river...I mean, really watch it? Are you aware that Timber Run could overpower us all? Well, it could. That river owns all the land beneath those little innocent-looking ripples and, if it decides that it wants more land, it will take it," Roger said in a quiet, monotone voice. "We owe much to Noah Cutler. It was because of his respect, not only for the river, but the land adjacent to its banks, that we have this marvel of nature."

"Noah? Wasn't he the guy that built the ark?"

Roger rolled his eyes. "No, of course not," a disgusted Roger spit out. "Noah Cutler was a wealthy man who owned much of Elk Mountain at one time. He needed to get his cargo of logs to the sawmill some thirty miles away. He didn't want to pollute the water by using coal burning boats, so he created a way to use the power of mules. He rigged them to the side of the barges and walked them along the banks. Those dumb animals pulled the barges down Timber Run to the sawmill. It wasn't until he lost the easement to use the land alongside the river that he used steam-driven barges. In fact, it was because of his dogmatic loyalty to keeping the river pure, that Timber Run is still one of the cleanest waterways in the nation," Roger explained in a surprisingly patient manner. "While Cutler County is no longer known for lumbering, it's still the headquarters for the Riverton Lumber Company."

"I'm not sure where you're coming from, Roger," Henry said, revealing his impatience. "Why should I know all this stuff?"

Roger sighed deeply. "You have never learned to listen. It's difficult to teach a jackass anything. You're like those mules who pulled the barges—doomed. A man who doesn't know history has little power. Riverton has a rich history. For instance, didn't you ever wonder why all of the original streets in Riverton are named after trees? You pathetic creature, you need to be educated."

Henry opened his mouth to argue, but thought better of it.

"We need to have a talk. But, before I start, I want you to know that I know what you have been up to. No, shutting your eyes won't help. If you come clean—and I mean this—if you come clean, you'll make out like a bandit. If you don't—then you and I will no longer be doing business together," Roger said without even looking at Henry. He suddenly grabbed Henry's arm and said sharply, "Now talk! I know that you're blackmailing my family. How dare you do that to any Fadden? You weasel, you."

Henry's arm was hurting and he tried to pull away. Roger turned his head and finally looked at the frightened man who had turned white. "I understand," Henry said, trying to sound normal.

"First, I want to know how much you got and from whom. You have lots to gain, providing I get the truth," Roger said icily. "With whom did you start, what did you find, and how much did you get?"

Henry swallowed hard. "I began with Joshua. He's gay. His lover is Morgan Truesdale, a well-known composer and pianist. Apparently, they've been able to keep their relationship private. He paid me 10K."

Henry was surprised that Roger didn't change the expression on his face. "Then, I focused on Crystal. That one's fairly complex. It seems that when she was just fifteen, and as high as a kite, she was driving her daddy's car, when she hit and killed two toddlers, who had been playing in a sandbox in their yard. Because of her age, all records were sealed. That happened when the family was living in upper New York. They then moved to Riverton where her daddy kept her under control for several years before she met and married your nephew. Her name was Lilly, but her parents changed it to Crystal when they moved here. I couldn't find any evidence that your nephew knows anything about his wife's past. I got 10K out of her. Look, Roger, I'll give them their money back. I was just wanted…"

"I know what you were trying to do. What about the other two?"

Henry took a deep breath, "Well, Mary Jo is having an affair with a married guy named Darius Davis, who has two kids and a pregnant wife. I didn't get any money from her, yet. So far, I haven't found out anything about Greg, but he seems to have lots of different bank accounts. Seems like you have a very busy family."

Roger was stroking his beard. He suddenly realized that Henry might be planning on using all the information he has uncovered to shake him down, too. He needed to act quickly to protect his family and himself. Without missing a beat, in his head he formed the perfect plan to prevent that from happening. "Henry, how would you like to be on the inside?"

"Inside what?"

"My little group. You've told me the truth, so I want to reward you. You must stop your extortion schemes, but you'll make a hundred times that if you play your cards right. Make sure I get all the paperwork you have amassed during your investigations…and I mean **ALL**. Do you agree?" Roger asked sharply.

"Of course. Here are my files and I'll give you my notebook, too. Am I really a part of your group?" Henry asked as if he couldn't believe his good luck.

Roger casually looked through the paperwork Henry had placed in his lap. He picked up two of the photos, looked them over, and then shoved them back into the pile.

"Do you remember when you delivered a package to a guy named Horse?" Henry nodded. "Well, Horse and I want to make you one of our partners. We want you to keep your office open and take on only simple cases. Also, Horse wants you to learn how to dress like a winner. He says he wants you to get rid of your sloppy clothes and make sure you shine your shoes. In this shopping bag is a package wrapped as a Christmas present. All you have to do is get on the 4:00 pm bus to Pittsburgh with the shopping bag. When you get to Pittsburgh, don't go into the terminal—they have cameras in there. Horse and a guy named Ziggy will meet you there. They'll be in an RV on the parking lot across the street from the bus terminal. You can't miss the RV since it has a Steelers Fan banner attached to the rear window. Give the shopping bag to Horse, and he'll give you a package. Get the next bus back to Riverton and don't open your package until you are home. You'll probably have to make this trip two or three times a month. Are you willing to do this?"

"What will be in my package?" Henry asked excitedly.

"Each time it may be different amounts, but it will be a lot more money than you are getting out of my family. Our group demands loyalty. This is your opportunity to be part of the Big Time, Henry. Now don't blow it! Take your shopping bag and get out of here on the double. And, for God's sake, take care of all that money," Roger ordered.

"One question. Why can't I just use my car? I hate buses."

"Oh, Henry, use your head. When you drive a car to Pittsburgh, it could be caught on cameras at lots of places—gas stations, food joints, turnpike toll booths. For God's sake, Henry, wise up," Roger said gruffly. "Now, scram."

Roger couldn't help chuckling as he watched the dumb ass waddle down Hemlock Street. It was so easy getting what he wanted out of the so-called detective. The guy was so stupid that he kind of felt sorry for him. But, business was business and anyone who knew too much about his family, must go. Nice and clean, just like the dead Indian. He didn't want to know how Horse would get rid of the problem—he only wanted it done tonight.

CHAPTER 17

H ENRY STRUGGLED UP the steps that led to his office. He felt different. Now he was part of a "syndicate—something he had always wanted. Money was going to come rolling in. His head was spinning. He had to get ready for his bus ride, but, meanwhile, he had to hide a few things.

Standing on a chair, he reached up and took down the picture of George Washington that was on the wall behind his desk. He liked this piece of art since his sister had given it to him as a gift when he opened his office. He laid the picture face down on his desk and began to peel off some of the brown paper that covered the back. Then, he took all the Fadden information that he hadn't given to Roger and slid each photo and document under the paper. After he resealed the paper, he put the picture back on the wall. Now, if Roger sent anyone to check Henry's office, they won't find anything that would upset the apple cart.

It was time to go shopping. His first stop was the leather shop on Plum Street. As he stepped into the little corner shop, he couldn't wait until he could start trying on one of those beautiful leather jackets that were displayed in the window. As the salesman took one jacket after another off the rack, Henry was thrilled with the attention he was getting. It was a difficult decision to make, but he finally chose a black, calves skin with a red lining. When the salesman offered to place the jacket in a garment bag, Henry decided to wear the coat immediately.

As Henry opened the door to leave the shop, the salesman called after him, "Oh, sir, you left your shopping bag in the dressing room!"

Henry swallowed hard. His face turned red and he scurried back in, grabbed the bag and hurried out the door. After his nerves calmed down, he decided to purchase a pair of shoes. After all, if Horse was going to be his friend, he needed to please the man who could easily tear him in half.

It seemed like forever until the bus was ready to leave Riverton. Henry was pleased that there were only about seven or eight people boarding the bus. He didn't want to have to share a seat with anyone. He quickly chose a seat, settled in against the window, and put the shopping bag on the seat beside him.

"Oh, my, someone's getting a big Christmas present," a lady said as she looked at the bag. "I hope Santa is that good to me."

Henry just smiled. He didn't want to talk with anyone. He wanted to focus on what to say to Horse and Ziggy. He curled up in the corner of his seat with his legs wrapped around the shopping bag and closed his eyes. When the bus hit a bump, he jumped and opened his eyes wide. He was surprised to see that it was snowing steadily. That damned Roger was right. He breathed a sigh of relief when the bus pulled into the terminal. He grabbed the bag and made his way off the bus. He immediately saw the parking lot and ran across the street. At first, he couldn't see the RV and began to panic, but then he spied the Steelers banner. With a shaky hand, he knocked on the door.

"Hello, Henry," Horse said. "We've been waiting for you. This here, this ugly little bugger, his name is Ziggy. Daddy Bear said you'd be coming."

"Daddy Bear?"

"Yeah. You know him as Roger," Horse laughed. "You know, Henry, we need another name for you. You have a preference?"

Henry stood there with his mouth open.

"How about Einstein?" Horse suggested.

"Einstein?" Henry repeated.

"Yeah, Daddy Bear said you're damned smart and Einstein was very smart."

"Well, okay," Henry said as he allowed himself to smile. "How did you get your name?"

Ziggy jumped up and said, "Are you sure you want to know?" he asked Henry. Not waiting for an answer, he said, "He used to make his money by doing away with expensive race horses when they started going downhill and the owners wanted to collect on the insurance. Horse knew how to make it look like the damned animal died of a heart attack," Ziggy said as he grabbed this throat and pretended to drop over.

When Ziggy slid behind the driver's seat and turned the motor on, Henry said, "Hey, guys, I need to catch the next bus back to Riverton. Did you forget?"

"We're going to move the RV, Einstein. We don't want to be seen here too long. We'll have you back here before the bus leaves for Riverton. Oh, and that bag over there. That's yours, you lucky dog, you. Just relax. We have a couple of hours. Meanwhile, how about a beer?" Horse said as he opened the refrigerator.

Henry couldn't help notice the rings that Horse was wearing on his gigantic hands. He had two diamond rings on each hand. "That's some bling you have on, Horse," Henry said.

"Well, I like how they make me feel," Horse replied as he held out his hands so that Henry could get a better look.

"This sure is a nice RV. One could live very comfortably in it all year round," Henry said as he looked over some of the items on the counter. "Wow, this is sure a big roll of plastic wrap," Henry said as he patted the roll with his hand. "What do you use that for?"

"Oh, I find uses for it," Horse said.

"He sure does," Ziggy said as he chuckled.

CHAPTER 18

I T WAS CHRISTMAS Day. Otto was sitting on the front steps of Roger's home to welcome the dinner guests as they arrived. Walter was rolling around in the snow, having a good time. Otto was a bit sleepy since he had gotten up very early that morning to go to church service with Roger. He was proudly wearing a bright red scarf that Santa had left for him under the huge tree that sat in the far corner of the spacious dining room. Worried that Walter might be getting cold, Otto opened his jacket and pulled Walter onto his lap and covered him the best he could.

"Walter, I'll share my jacket with you," he said as he strained his eyes to see if any cars were entering the driveway. When he spotted Mary Jo's car, Otto jumped with joy. "Mary Jo's coming. Beth and Greg are in the car, too. Now, mind your manners today, Walter."

Walter scooted out of Otto's lap and ran directly to Mary Jo, who made a big fuss over him. "Merry Christmas, Walter. Oh, Otto, did Santa bring you that pretty scarf? It makes you look handsome," Mary Jo said as she headed up the sidewalk.

"I wanted to make a snowman, but Roger said that it wouldn't work with this little bit of snow," Otto said sadly.

"I heard that Pittsburgh got sixteen inches," Mary Jo told Otto. "That would be plenty of snow for a snowman."

Beth, who was playing with Walter, said, "Tell you what, Otto. If it snows again before I go back to college, I'll come over here, and we'll build a whole family of snowmen."

As Beth and Otto discussed the details, Joshua and Crystal, pulled in behind Mary Jo's car. Crystal hurried past Otto and Walter as fast as she could. Joshua pulled off his gloves and patted Walter a few times. "She didn't waste any time getting in to see Uncle Roger, now, did she?" Joshua said quietly to Greg.

As the family filed out of the cloakroom, Roger escorted them into the Grand Room that was decorated in gold and white. He had read in a magazine that Donald Trump had used the same colors in his apartment and it made Roger feel powerful to replicate something that a billionaire had. "As you can see, I have arranged the chairs in a circle. I thought it would be nice to be able to see all of you since we really don't get together like this very often."

"Uncle Roger," Crystal said sweetly, "this room is simply divine. You have such excellent taste in all things."

As hors d'oeuvres and eggnog were served, Roger said, "I'm expecting two more guests—Cindy and Russ Grove. When I was in church this morning, I heard that Cindy's mother had had her appendix removed last night and is still in the hospital. So, I thought it would be nice to invite them to join us for dinner. Cindy's mother has been our organist for many years and does so much for our church." He didn't mention that he thought it was a good time to get to know Russ better, especially since Roger was looking for ways to get some special deliveries dropped off near the Mexican border—Russ and his tractor-trailer might come in handy.

Just as the family settled in, Teresa, Roger's housekeeper, ushered an embarrassed Cindy and Russ into the Grand

Room. "Mr. Fadden, please excuse us for being late, but we stopped by the hospital to check on Cindy's mom," Russ said as he and Cindy joined the group.

"I hope she's doing well," Roger said in a gentle tone.

Cindy smiled. "Mom's doing fine. Right now she just wants to sleep. We'll be bringing her home tomorrow."

"It's good to hear that she's doing fine. But, how disappointed she must be to miss Christmas Day with her family," Mary Jo said.

"You two have arrived just in time for our little Christmas Day ritual," Roger said.

"Mr. Fadden," Russ said, "Cindy and I can leave the room to give you more privacy."

"No, no, please stay. Santa has something for everyone," Roger said as he beamed. "Now, folks, I want to begin with Beth. My dear, I don't know if you have made up your mind about what you want to do as far as your career is concerned. I will not urge you one way or the other, but I want you to know that there always will be a place for you with Fadden Insurance and Investments. If you join the company, Uncle Joshua will take you under his wing and teach you the business from the ground up."

"Uncle Roger, you old fox," Greg said as he laughed. "No urging?"

"Of course, Papa Roger, I want to work for you. I also have an offer to flip burgers at Burger King, but I plan to turn that offer down," Beth said as she got up and hugged Roger who was now smiling broadly.

"Otto, my friend, you are next. You never let me down. You have taken good care of Walter. Here is your envelope. I want you to meet with Joshua who will help you plan your budget for next year. He tells me that you have done a fine job with your money this year. And, I must say, that Walter is the best-dressed dog in town," Roger said as they all laughed.

"Greg and Joshua, as far as you and your wives are concerned, I have added a little something to your envelopes." They were all hanging onto Roger's every word. "While you are all used to getting a check from me, you also will find a letter in your Christmas envelope. Each letter is unique. Please don't open your envelopes until you get home. Greg. Joshua, Mary Jo, and Crystal: you may or may not chose to share your letter with your spouses—it is entirely your choice. I have tried, over the years, to stay out of your personal lives. Lately, however, I have become concerned over several matters. So, read your letters carefully and consider my recommendations. Rest assured, I consider the matters closed and you may make your own decisions."

Mary Jo's heart skipped a beat. All she could think about was that somehow Roger may have found out about Darius. Her hands began to tremble. She was unaware that Crystal had to take several deep breaths to keep from fainting—her past may have finally caught up with her with a vengeance. Joshua immediately thought that his relationship with Morgan might be in jeopardy and Roger might remove him from the company. If he is, Joshua vowed that he would hunt down that sonofabitch who blackmailed him. Greg couldn't imagine what was going to be in his letter. He and Roger had always gotten along and Greg didn't have any skeletons in his closet that Roger would find objectionable.

"And now, Cindy and Russ: Santa hasn't forgotten you two," Roger said as he looked at the Groves. "I checked our company files that indicate that you have your car, your home, and your truck all insured with us. As a gift from Santa, your fees are paid for all of the coming year."

"Mr. Fadden, I can't let you do that. I..."

"It's done. Just let this old man have his way," Roger said as he raised his hand in the air. "I have recently made a few changes in my will. When I am gone, I don't want any fussing or fighting over property. Of course, the office building stays with the company. My home, however, is another matter." Roger took a sip of his eggnog and paused for a few minutes. "I want either Greg or Joshua to buy my home. I'm sure that you two can come to some agreement. I have one stipulation—no changes may be made to the structure or the grounds around the home for a period of twenty years."

"You realize, Uncle Roger, such a stipulation may be difficult to follow. However, I'm certain that the two of us will be able to make certain that your wishes are followed," Greg said as he nodded to Joshua.

"But, what about the dead Indian?" Otto asked.

"The what?" Crystal questioned.

"A long time ago, there were Indians in Riverton and one of them is buried underneath the rose bushes," Otto said, proud that he was now the center of attention.

"Otto and I have our own little secrets, don't we Otto?" Roger said as he winked at Otto.

"Oh, yes sir, we do," Otto replied as he winked back. "We have our secrets."

"Folks, let's move to the dining room. Teresa and the florists worked on the decorations for two days. You will be amazed at what she has done," Roger said.

As Mary Jo entered the dining room, she was taken aback at the sight before her eyes. In the center of the huge, mahogany table was an exquisite arrangement of pink and red roses that was complimented by a single rose at each place setting. In the corner, behind Roger's chair, pink, red and shiny silver balls were interspersed among hundreds and hundreds of twinkling white lights on a huge Douglas fir. An ornate fireplace dominated the far end of the room. The long mantle was decorated with a dozen LED candles, bringing attention to the red velvet bows and enormous pine cones nestled in a lush garland. A crackling fire completed the effect. Mary Jo was spellbound.

When Roger entered the room, he said, "Ah, I see you're admiring Teresa's work. As usual, she was in charge of the decorating. She is amazing, don't you think? You should have heard her bossing the florist and his crew around."

"You mean there's more behind those long, white aprons and orthopedic shoes than a mere cook?" Crystal said as she smirked.

Roger was perturbed by Crystal's remark but held his tongue.

"Uncle Roger, this room is gorgeous. I may never want to leave," Mary Jo said as she moved closer to the tree. "And, I assume that's Walter's spot," she said as she pointed to a large cushion just a few feet away from the tree.

As everyone took their seats, Crystal turned her head abruptly as she saw Walter enter the room. "Certainly, you don't allow *him* in here while we are eating, do you?"

"Yes, we do. Settle down, Crystal, or I just might have him bite you," Roger tried to tease the uptight woman. "Russ, do you participate in the Make-a-Wish truck convoy?"

"I sure do. I love to see the kids enjoying themselves as they pull the air horn cords in the trucks as we drive down the expressway. Last year, we had over 100 trucks of all sizes in the convoy. I had a ten-year-old boy in my truck, who couldn't stop thanking me for allowing him to ride next to me," Russ said as he reached up in the air as if he were pulling on an air horn.

"That's it! Russ, that's the favor I want from you. Take me for a ride in your truck some time and let me pull the horn," Roger said excitedly.

"Oh, oh," Otto said, "May I come, too?"

"That will be fine. You can even bring Walter along," Russ added.

Otto jumped up, ran over to Walter and hugged him. "Did you hear that, Walter? We're going for a ride in a big truck!"

"Merry Christmas, everyone!" Roger said joyfully. He couldn't remember a Christmas that he had enjoyed as much as he was enjoying this one. There just might be something worthwhile in being a nice guy.

CHAPTER 19

As MORGAN WAS adjusting his tie, he said, "Well, was Uncle Roger his usual miserable self on Christmas Day?"

"No. In fact, he was quite remarkable," Joshua said with a smile on his face. "How was your holiday?"

"I was restless the whole day. I can't wait until we no longer have to play this silly game of hide and seek by not being seen anywhere together," Morgan pouted.

"I have a late Christmas present for you, my love. Tonight we're going out."

"What did you say? I don't think I heard that right," Morgan said as he turned away from the mirror with a surprised look on his face.

"Anywhere you want to go and *yes,* you heard correctly."

Morgan threw his arms around Joshua. "Tell me again," he said coyly. "What about Uncle Roger?"

"It's his idea," Joshua said as Morgan playfully fell on the sofa.

"Will wonders never cease?"

"In the envelope with my usual Christmas check, Roger wrote a detailed note. He said I should tell Crystal, divorce her, and make a life with you. I'm not certain if he simply hates Crystal more than he does gays, or if he has had some type of epiphany, but I'll take it either way," Joshua said as he kept an eye on Morgan who seemed as if he was in shock.

"Why now? What brought this on?" a bewildered Morgan asked.

"I really don't know. He was almost joyful as he explained that he had written each one of us a note to go along with our checks. And, he said that it was up to us if we wanted to share our letters with anyone. As soon as we got home, Crystal took her envelope into her dressing room and closed the door. When she came out, she was obviously upset, so I thought she had learned about us, but she didn't say a word. I asked her if she was okay and she fluffed me off as if nothing happened. So…I told her."

"No! You mean she knows about us?" Morgan said as he put his hand over his mouth. "And, then what happened?"

"Funny, there were no tears. No shouting or raving—just silence. After a few minutes, she merely said that she would see an attorney in a few days, and she felt that she and I could come to an agreement on property division."

As this information sunk in, Joshua and Morgan stood mute. The ticking of the mantle clock created a dramatic moment that seemed to awaken Morgan to the reality. He began to smile. Then his smile became broader.

Morgan finally shouted, "I want to go dancing—no, dinner *and* dancing. My friends won't be shocked, but yours may well be," Morgan reminded Joshua.

"I'm curious, though. I'd like to know what was in Crystal's letter," Joshua said and Morgan took his hand.

"We don't need to know," Morgan assured Joshua. "We've been waiting a long time for this. Your attorney will guide you through the divorce process. Meanwhile, I'll take care of making room in this apartment for one more person. Oh, my God, our time has finally come."

"By the way, what are you doing New Year's Eve?" Joshua asked nonchalantly as he handed Morgan a gilt-edged invitation.

Morgan opened the envelope slowly. He held it up to his eyes and kept staring at the elegant script. "No! Damn! The Midnight Ball at Cutler Mansion! How did you...when...did you...impossible..."

"I have my sources. Now you have some place where you can wear your brand new tux to show off your dance moves. Did you forget that I'm good friends with Sylvester Latrobe, the chairman of this special event? His great-great-great grandfather,"—he paused for a few seconds, and then went on—"I think that's the right number of *greats*, built the Cutler Mansion. The ballroom is unique. The walls are covered with beautiful carvings created by the immigrants who worked there so many years ago. The mansion is the biggest, most prominent edifice on Cherry Blossom Lane." Joshua started laughing when Morgan began to dance around the living room.

Suddenly, Morgan stopped dancing. He stood still for a few seconds before the tears began to flow. Joshua jumped up and took Morgan in his arms. "We're free, Morgan, we're free."

⤳ CHAPTER 20 ⤶

M ARY JO HAD had an upset stomach ever since Roger had handed her that envelope. She had known what it would say. Remarkably, Greg had never said a word about Roger's actions on Christmas Day. Perhaps it would be better if she never opened it. But, then again, depending on how much Roger actually knew, she couldn't continue to ignore the stupid thing. And, there was always the possibility that Roger didn't know about Darius. She waited until she heard Greg pull out of the driveway before she slid her letter opener under the seal of the envelope that could radically change her life. She held her breath.

A check for five thousand dollars lay on top—Roger's usual Christmas gift. Slowly, she unfolded the letter. She allowed each word to sink in before she glanced at the next one. He knew it all. But, when she came to the last line, she thought she would pass out. She read it aloud—*"I am surprised that you would choose a lover who is married with two small children and another one on the way."* Darius had told her many times that he and Ellen lived separate lives—and that it would only be a few more months until he could leave his young wife.

*Darius lied to me...he lied to me...*went through her mind like a bolt of lightning. She had believed his every word, but they were all lies.

Roger had not threatened to reveal what he knew to Greg. He didn't order her to tell her husband. But, she couldn't take her eyes off the final sentence. It was only a few weeks ago when she and Darius had talked about how many more months they had to wait until Ellen would agree to a divorce. Mary Jo wanted to pick up the phone and let Darius know what a bastard he was; but how would that change things?

"Cindy. I need Cindy," Mary Jo said out loud as she reached for her phone.

On the third ring, Cindy answered. "I need you, Cindy, I need you now. My world just blew up in my face," Mary Jo said as she began to cry. "No, don't come here. I don't know when Greg will be back. Meet me at the *Magical Garden Café*. Good, I'm on my way."

As she stepped into the trendy new restaurant, she was relieved to see that it was not crowded. There were several workers changing the décor from the holidays to Valentine's Day, but one of the private gazebos was not occupied. So Mary Jo hurried over and slid into the seat. While the plants and flowers were breath-taking, Mary Jo was unable to appreciate their beauty and propped her head on her hands as she leaned on the table.

Suddenly, Cindy was by her side. "Mary Jo, what happened?" she asked as she tossed her handbag on the bench.

Mary Jo told Cindy about the letter Uncle Roger included in her Christmas envelope. "Here, I'll let you read it," Mary Jo said as she placed the wrinkled sheet of paper in front Cindy.

When she had finished reading it, Cindy said, "Okay. Now let's examine it carefully. Are you more upset over the fact the Darius' wife is pregnant, or that Uncle Roger knows about the affair?" she asked as she took Mary Jo's hand in hers.

"What?" Mary Jo said sharply as she pulled her hand away.

"Look, if you want my help, you'll have to tell me how you really feel. I want to help you, Mary Jo. You called me."

"You're right. You're right. Darius lied to me. He told me that he and Ellen were no longer sleeping together. He lied to me."

"Did you tell him that you were still sleeping with Greg?" Cindy questioned.

Mary Jo sat quietly for a minute or two. "Well, I'm still married to him."

"And he's still married to Ellen. Now, come on, sweetie, get off that righteous horse and get real. In this letter, Roger doesn't threaten to tell anyone. Why do you think he didn't?"

Mary Jo shook her head. "I don't know. I also don't know if he told Greg about my affair in the letter that he wrote to him. I can't be sure that Greg doesn't know. All I know is that, when Greg read his letter, he chuckled, folded it back up, and never said a word to me about it."

"Let's assume that Greg doesn't know. Do you plan on telling him?"

"That's a tough one. I'm not sure."

"Here's a really tough one...what do you plan on doing about Darius?"

Mary Jo closed her eyes. "I should tell him it's over. I should smack him until his teeth rattle. I should stomp on his heart like he did to mine. But I do know that I will not continue our relationship unless he leaves her now. I'm not going to wait until another child grows up and enters first grade."

"Have you thought it might be possible that he has had no intention of ever leaving Ellen?"

Mary Jo lowered her head. She was lost in thought. Cindy knew her friend very well, so she sat quietly and gave Mary Jo time to think about that possibility.

"I used to think that he loved me as much as I loved him. I felt so special. Here was a romantic, handsome man who supposedly was madly in love with me. He made me feel as if I were walking on air," Mary Jo said softly. "I ignored being put aside so many times because of his family commitments. I told myself that that was the price I had to pay for getting involved with a married man. While I worried about someday having to tell Beth, I hardly gave any thought to Greg. Does that make me a horrible person? Greg has taken good care of me for so long, but I just tossed his feelings aside. But, maybe, just maybe, I might not have to tell him at all."

"If you break it off with Darius or not, you need to be the one to tell Greg. However, I recommend that you talk with Darius. At least, listen to what he has to say. Remember, while he did lie to you, you also told quite a few lies, too. Think about the lies you told Greg. Get in touch with Darius. But, I think it advisable for you to consult with Pastor Diebert and get his advice."

"Cindy, I know the right thing to do—I just can't bring myself to do it."

Just then the waitress appeared and placed menus on the table. Cindy quickly said, "We'll each have black coffee and share a sticky bun with pecans."

Mary Jo had her eyes closed, as she tried desperately to make her heartache go away. She couldn't look at her friend. She wasn't sure that she was ashamed of herself, or whether she was sorry that her torrid romance was over.

"When was the last time you saw Darius?" Cindy asked.

"A few weeks before Christmas. We only got together when we had STAIRS meetings," Mary Jo responded. Then, she added, "The January meeting was cancelled due to the snow storm."

"If you and Darius are so madly in love, you two couldn't arrange some time to see one another? You've got to be kidding,"

Cindy said as she cut the bun in half. "Do you want yours buttered?"

Mary Jo shook head and slowly took a sip of her coffee. "Okay, I'll follow your advice and give him a call. In fact, I'll do it now."

Cindy got up quickly and walked away.

"Mr. Davis, please," Mary Jo said nervously. "Mrs. Fadden calling."

"Hello, Mrs. Fadden, nice to hear from you. How were your holidays?"

"We need to talk. This is important," Mary Jo practically whispered into the phone.

"I'm booked today. Will tomorrow be okay?"

"No. I want to see you today," Mary Jo insisted. "Or, are you too busy buying baby clothes?" she said as she cupped her hand around her mouth.

After a long pause, Darius said, "Oh, I see. Alright. I can meet you at our warehouse at two."

"Fine, I'll be there," Mary Jo said as she tried to calm down. She closed her eyes and leaned back on the plush seat. When she sensed that Cindy had returned and put her arm around Mary Jo's shoulder, she looked up. "I'm meeting him at two."

Cindy sat still for a few minutes. "Let him talk, Mary Jo. Allow him to explain himself before you let him know about the pregnancy."

"He knows that I know...I asked him if he was too busy to meet me because he was buying baby clothes," Mary Jo said as she looked up to the ceiling.

"Oh, but I still recommend that you allow him to speak first. Look, you knew that something would happen that would force you to make a decision. It just came along sooner than you expected. Put your big-girl panties on and face it. You know that I'll be here for you. Now, get out of here and face the music."

CHAPTER 21

G REG COULDN'T BELIEVE that Roger knew all about his bank accounts, even the ones overseas. However, his uncle wasn't upset with him. In fact, he indicated that he was proud that Greg was smart enough to hide a great deal of money. After all, he said in his note, *"You'd get it when I'm gone anyway."* The only thing Greg couldn't understand was that Roger suggested that he pay more attention to Mary Jo. That comment surprised him because Greg was well aware that Roger never really liked her.

But, the biggest shock came when Joshua told him that Roger had recommended that he divorce Crystal and marry Morgan. While Crystal was sort of an odd-duck, Greg couldn't help but feel sorry for her. But, she had had to figure it all out long ago. While Greg had known for some time that his brother was gay, he was not prepared for Roger to accept a gay nephew. However, he felt that his uncle would like Morgan if he ever got to meet him. Greg thought that perhaps if he could get Roger to attend one of Morgan's concerts, he would more readily accept the talented man.

When he had questioned Mary Jo about the letter Roger had given to her, she said that he recommend that she work somewhere else other than a smelly dog pound. While he never knew Mary Jo to lie to him, her explanation about the contents of her letter didn't ring true. As he walked up the stairs to the second floor of their home, he suddenly began to think about looking for the letter among Mary Jo's possessions. He had never spied on his wife in all the years they were married. But now—now, he was beginning to feel a need to do just that.

If someone would ask him to define his relationship with Mary Jo, he would be hard pressed to say anything negative. Yet, deep in his guts, he knew that he didn't want anything different. His main interest in life was to build a fortune, an even bigger one than his Uncle Roger had. He had faith in his ability to do that—with or without a wife.

Roger's Christmas letters are rapidly changing things—especially for Joshua and Crystal. However, perhaps the ones Mary Jo and I received will do the same thing.

CHAPTER 22

E VER SINCE CRYSTAL had returned home after consulting with her lawyer, she had been roaming throughout the house. "My house," she said out loud. She wasn't particularly shocked when Joshua told her that there was someone else in his life, but she was flabbergasted that it was a male. All the years that her husband had left her alone, time after time, she had assumed that it was for some young, curvy woman who had him captivated—but a male pianist? But, it was what it was.

When he had told her yesterday that they needed to talk, she thought for sure that Roger had informed her husband about her accident and the toddlers that she had killed. She couldn't believe that even Roger, who could be spiteful to almost anyone, could have been as cruel as that. Joshua, however, never mentioned anything and seemed totally unaware of what she had done. Perhaps Joshua still didn't know. Crystal hoped to keep it that way—at least until Joshua had completed his promise to her to give her the house and a sizeable bank account. Her lawyer felt that Crystal could even get more than Joshua had already promised.

Crystal finally sat down on a lounge chair in her dressing room. She glanced around at the fashionable clothes that were all on white satin hangers. On the far side of the room were racks and racks of shoes and handbags, all with designer labels. And, she adored her ten-drawer jewelry case that stood beside the three-way mirror. While she was aware that Joshua was quite generous with his concessions, she had to make certain that she could maintain her lifestyle until someone else would come along to support her even more lavishly.

She allowed herself to think about possible easy marks who could fit the bill. The one person who immediately popped into her head was Sinclair Hancock, a retired CEO twenty years her senior. An extremely wealthy man, Sinclair was the catch of the year. While he was a bit on the conservative side, Crystal knew all too well the tricks of the trade to get his full attention. Crystal also knew that he had a weakness for brunettes. Since he had a sterling reputation, she had to make certain that her past be kept hidden. If she wanted to set her cap for Sinclair, she had all the right stuff. And, since Joshua had promised that he would pay her a monthly allowance for three years after their divorce was final, she could seek him out and ask for advice on handling her finances. It should be a piece of cake getting Sinclair to the altar.

Picking up her phone, she decided to call Sinclair. "Hello, Sinclair, this is Crystal Fadden...I was wondering if you would be able to meet me for lunch? I would like to run some financial decisions by you that I must make in the near future. You see, I filed for divorce today...No, not another woman, another man...Yes!...How sweet of you to say that, but I'm really worried about how to handle my finances and, well, since that is your area of expertise, I was hoping you would agree to be my patron...Oh, thank you, Sinclair, you are so understanding...Dinner?...Tomorrow night?...Sounds lovely, Sinclair...Do you mean the red dress I wore at last year's Valentine's dance?...How charming that you remembered it...

Of course, I'll be happy to wear it, Sinclair. Just for you…Seven will be fine…Sinclair, I'll see you then."

She jumped up and immediately took the dress off the rack. It was the red satin Vera Wang that had almost no back and fit like a glove. And, the fact that he remembered her in that sexy dress only worked to Crystal's advantage. A widower for over two years, Sinclair often was seen at various events, but always without a companion, so there was probably no competition at the moment. Crystal wiggled into the red dress and walked back and forth in front of the large three-way mirror. She was pleased with what she saw. *If this doesn't start Sinclair's motor running, nothing will.*

⤜❧ CHAPTER 23 ❧⤛

As MARY JO parked her car in front of the Davis Media warehouse, she still did not know what she was going to say to Darius. While she told herself that she hated him for what he had done, she knew that she loved him as much as ever. When she looked into her rearview mirror, she spied a Davis Media truck coming up the driveway. What if that's one of the employees? She held her breath. When she actually saw that it was, indeed, Darius, her anger returned once again.

Darius parked the truck and hurried over to Mary Jo's car and hopped in.

Before he even closed the door, he began talking. "Mary Jo, please don't be angry with me. When Ellen told me that she was pregnant, I just couldn't bring myself to tell you. Look at me, Mary Jo. I'm sorry," he said mournfully, as he tried to reach for her hand.

"You said that you two were living separate lives. You also told me that in another fifteen or so months, we could be together. Are you sorry for that, too?" Mary Jo said without turning her head.

"She came into my bedroom one night and..."

"Wow, are you going to give me a blow-by-blow description of your love-making abilities?" Mary Jo asked as she finally looked him in his eyes.

Mary Jo was breathing hard. Her anger was welling inside her like a volcano ready to erupt. She wanted to make him feel her pain. But, somehow, deep inside her, she realized that he would never be capable of such an emotion.

"Look, you need to face the reality of our situation," Darius pleaded.

"And, what does that mean?" Mary Jo said facetiously.

"You and I have something really special. Can't we just keep it that way for a while? We can have the best of both worlds. No one knows about us yet, so why not just keep on going with what we have?"

"You're honestly asking me to remain your mistress, while you go on procreating children with your *young* wife—at least until you have the number of kids you want? Is that what you're proposing?" Mary Jo asked as she raised her voice.

"Not exactly."

"Then, what do you mean?" Mary Jo said between clenched teeth.

"I just need a bit more time to get things straightened out at home," Darius said. "I can't walk out on her right now. Think of my children."

"You should have thought of them a long time ago. They're your kids, not mine. How dare you even say that to me?" Mary Jo paused to catch her breath and regain her composure. The pause lengthened into a long silence—long enough for her to realize that Darius would never change. She had been a fool. He was a bastard. She deserved better than this. "You're some piece of work, Darius," Mary Jo emphasized each word. "Get the hell out of my car."

"Mary Jo—listen to me," Darius begged. "I really love you."

"No, it's now or never. I don't like playing the role of a mistress. Get out!"

CHAPTER 24

HILDA HENDERSON DIDN'T like driving in the rain—especially in a downpour. Each time she hit a pot hole, as she drove down Hemlock Street, she shuddered. But, she had to find out why her brother never showed up on Christmas Day. She had waited several weeks before getting too concerned, since he had told her that he was working on a big case. She must have tried calling him over a hundred times—nothing. She was grateful to find a parking space in the lot alongside the building where her brother's office was located. As she scooted out of the car, she tried to protect her hair; after all, she had paid thirty dollars yesterday to get a cut and style and she wanted to get her money's worth. The wind was whipping around her frail body as she fought to prevent her umbrella from turning inside out. As she passed Barney's Sandwich Shop, a pudgy man behind the counter waved at her. When she pulled on the door handle that led to the back stairway to Henry's office, she shook the umbrella hard before she tucked it under her arm.

As she started up the steps, she suddenly experienced a feeling of dread. Her baby brother meant the world to her, and she felt as though she had let him down by not looking for him sooner. She stood in front of his office door and peered through the glass. She tried the doorknob and even shook it.

The office looked different. She didn't see any file cabinets. And, the chairs that Henry used to have lined up along one wall were gone. However, their dad's ugly, old desk was still there as well as the picture of George Washington hanging on the wall.

She decided to go back down the stairs and check with the man in the sandwich shop—perhaps he might know something about Henry. As she opened the door to the shop, a strong whiff of fried onions floated out the door.

"Excuse me, would you happen to know where my brother, Henry Henderson, is?" Hilda asked timidly.

"No. I haven't seen him since right before Christmas when he came by to pay his rent. He said he was going on a little trip. By the way, I'm Barney Fielding. I own this building."

"His office is different," Hilda said.

"Different? How?"

"Well, it looks as if he's moved. Even his little dish that's always filled with M&Ms is gone. But his desk is still there."

Barney reached under the counter and pulled out a ring of keys. "Let's go and check," he said as he led the way back upstairs. "I'm used to him not being around all the time. He even paid up his rent 'til the end of March," Barney said as he opened the office door. He stepped inside. "I'll be damned."

Hilda walked over to the desk and began to open the drawers—they were all empty. "I think my brother was robbed," she almost whispered.

Barney grabbed his cell phone. "Hey, Chief, I think we've had a robbery here at my place on the second floor...Okay, tell him to come right up."

In no time at all, they heard heavy footsteps. Barney opened the office door and greeted Winston Fulbright, a detective from the local precinct.

"When did you first notice that things were missing?" Detective Fulbright inquired.

"This here lady is Henry's sister. She came here today to find out why she couldn't get in touch with him since Christmas. She came and got me. I figured he was working on a case."

"Miss Henderson, I'll need you to come with me to the station to get detailed information from you. Meanwhile, Barney, don't let anyone in this office. I'll also need you to come down for questioning."

"But I got no idea where Henry is. If there was a robbery, it had to have happened on a Monday 'cause that's when I have my shop closed. Or else, I would have saw the stuff being taken out. That's all I know," Barney insisted.

"Well, I'll want to question you, anyway. It won't take long," Fulbright said.

"May I take that picture with me? I gave that to my brother as a good luck piece. Funny, I guess it really wasn't good luck, was it?" Hilda asked forlornly.

"I can't let you take anything—this may be a crime scene," Fulbright said.

Hilda responded, "My God, you think he's dead?"

"Sorry, Miss Henderson. I meant, it could have been a burglary. I didn't say anything about murder."

"Something terrible must have happened. Henry simply wouldn't go away this long without calling me. He just wouldn't," Hilda said with a tremor in her voice.

As the three of them left Henry's office, Fulbright said, "Barney, I'm gonna put tape over this door. I don't want you to bring anyone in here—no new tenants and such."

"Henry's paid up 'til the end of March," Barney said.

"How about a woman?" Fulbright asked.

"I never seen him with a woman—that don't say there weren't none—especially since he was in the investigation business," Barney offered as he raised his bushy eyebrows. "But, private detectives always seem to have good-looking women, wearing slouchy hats, around them."

"Barney, you watch way too many NCIS shows," Fulbright said as he left the building with Hilda.

⤙ CHAPTER 25 ⤚

I T WAS TWO days before Valentine's Day and Mary Jo was preparing to go to a meeting about STAIRS. She was morose. Darius had still not tried to get in touch with her, and she was determined not to call him. She wasn't certain how she was going to handle sitting near him at the meeting. After she made sure that everyone at the animal shelter knew what their assignments were for the day, she headed for her car. Just then, Mitch pulled up.

"I brought you a bag of a new kind of dog food that's supposed to be great for puppies. Their salesman gave me two bags, so I thought you might want to see whether your little pups like it," Mitch said, as he hoisted a bag from his truck bed and carried it inside.

"Mary Jo, how about you ride with me to the meeting today. No sense taking two cars. And, just maybe I can talk you into having lunch with me," Mitch said hopefully. "I want to hear more about Walter."

Mary Jo was grateful for the offer. "Okay. Thanks for the dog food. You're always so thoughtful."

Mitch opened the door of his truck and helped Mary Jo get in. "Madam," he smiled and said playfully, "your chariot awaits."

His smile was infectious enough that despite her dour

mood, she smiled back. "Otto is so excited that Walter will be the host for David's Dancing Dogs. He wanted something special for Walter to wear, so we went online and he chose a top hat and a wrap-around cape that has sparkles all over. Now he wants a platform for Walter to stand on. Can you help him with that?" Mary Jo asked.

"Sure can. The last time we met, Darius said that he could help in getting permission for me to take some of my animals to the park for our adoption plan. I thought we could use the old ark I have parked in the barn. I can divide the space into quarters. That way the animals won't be too crowded. Has he said anything further about this to you?"

Mary Jo took a deep breath. "I haven't seen Darius lately, but he'll probably be at the meeting today. What four animals were you thinking of putting in the ark?"

"Well, I have Cleopatra—a pigmy goat, whose one leg is shorter than the other, but she's very friendly. I thought Romeo might be a hit—he's a peacock who limps badly and loves to show off his feathers. Then, we have the Professor— my beautiful albino owl that can't fly. Last, but not least, is Sir Galahad—my miniature horse, who is blind, but gets around fairly well," Mitch explained. "Oh, I forgot, I may be getting twin baby donkeys. Seems there's a farm that may be going into bankruptcy and they would like to get rid of the donkeys since one is badly handicapped. They don't want to put him down, so they thought of me. They also believe that they won't grow very big—some kind of problem with growth hormones. I understand that they don't want the donkeys separated."

"When the kids see them, they'll go crazy," Mary Jo said as she relaxed for the first time today.

As they entered the meeting room, Crystal called out to Mary Jo. "Mary Jo, may I speak with you in private?"

"I'll meet you inside," Mitch said as he walked away.

"I guess you know that Joshua and I will be divorcing. Did you know that your brother-in-law is gay?" Crystal sniffed as she rolled her eyes.

"No. I'm sorry to hear about the divorce," Mary Jo said.

"Sinclair Hancock is serving as my financial advisor. He's so kind and thoughtful."

Mary Jo couldn't help but smile. She was certain that it wouldn't be too long before Crystal would lasso Sinclair at the altar. Mary Jo took Crystal's hand and said, "I wish you the best."

"Mary Jo, oh, Mary Jo," the director called out. "Darius won't be at the meeting today. His wife has had a miscarriage, and she's in intensive care. Isn't that sad?"

⋙ CHAPTER 26 ⋘

O TTO WAS SITTING in the kitchen eating an Oreo cookie, while Walter was lying right outside the doorway. "Teresa, where did Roger go?"

"He's an elder in the church and they're having their monthly meeting tonight," Teresa said as she put the cookie jar back on the counter.

"Is that important?" Otto asked.

"To Roger? My, yes. He serves the church very well. Otto, are you going to watch the fireworks tonight? The ballpark is celebrating their new field and they're going to shoot off lots of fireworks," Teresa said.

"Nah, we can't go. Walter's still limping a lot from the cut when he stepped on that piece of glass the other day. I guess we'll miss them," Otto said sadly.

"I have an idea. Why don't you and Walter sit out on the second floor balcony? You'll be able to see the fireworks from there," Teresa suggested.

"Will that be okay?" Otto asked hopefully.

"Sure. Be certain to keep Walter on the balcony with you. I'm going next door to play cards, but I'll be back by ten or so," Teresa said.

As soon as Teresa left, Otto jumped off his chair and almost fell on Walter. "We're gonna watch fireworks, Walter. Come,

Walter, come," Otto said as he hurried down the hallway and up the backstairs. When they neared the doorway to the balcony, Otto put the leash on Walter. "Now, Walter, this is just to keep you safe. I don't want you to fall off. So, I'll hold you on my lap."

Otto didn't mind waiting. He felt like he was a king in a castle, sitting on the balcony, overlooking his kingdom. When darkness finally came, and, before he knew it, the sky was filled with red, blue and white lights of different shapes. He was enthralled. He never had had a seat this good for fireworks in his whole life.

"Walter, that's all. Wasn't that great?" Otto guided Walter back inside and made certain that the door was closed tightly. Then, he noticed another door that didn't look like any of the others. He wondered if it was another bedroom. He tugged on the knob and the door opened. It surely wasn't a bedroom—it had no carpet and the room was filled with trunks and cartons. He couldn't see much even though he stretched his neck as far as he could. He felt around the inside of the doorway and found a light switch.

"Oh, this is really neat, Walter," Otto said as he sat down on the floor. Hanging on to Walter with one hand, he slowly opened the lid of one of the trunks. "Look, Walter, it's a toy train—with lots of cars. Oh, Walter, this is really cool. I wonder if Roger knows about this place." Otto then pulled out a jacket that had fancy gold buttons on it. Otto counted them. "I love this jacket, Walter. It looks like a real soldier's jacket. Ten brass buttons down the front and stripes on the sleeves. And, it's blue. I'll take this down with me, and when I see Roger, I'll ask him if I may have it."

When they got all the way down to Otto's basement apartment, Otto said, "Did you have fun tonight, Walter? I sure did!"

❧ CHAPTER 27 ❧

A S ROGER WAS finishing his breakfast, Teresa told him that she had given Otto permission to sit on the balcony to watch last night's fireworks. "I hope that was alright, Roger. I felt so sorry for Otto."

"Teresa, that was fine. I never would have thought of that—see how clever you are?" Roger said as he opened the newspaper to the obituaries. "We old folks have to check these every day to see whether our names are included," Roger said as he chuckled. "I often wonder how many people are also looking for *my* name."

"That's a terrible thing to say. We all love you, Roger," Teresa said as she began loading the dishwasher.

Just then, Otto came into the kitchen with the jacket, which he had found in the attic, draped over his arm. "Roger, look what I found," Otto said happily.

Roger's first instinct was to be angry. At one time, he had fun wearing that jacket, but when he saw it now, he only thought of what he had done that terrible night so long ago. Only one person knew. And, as long as Roger was breathing, that's the way he wanted it to remain. The jacket was only a copy of one that a Union soldier would have worn during the Civil War. However, at the present time, as he gazed at it, he didn't see a military uniform, but rather a symbol of darkness. The brass buttons, running down the front of the jacket, reflected the fluorescent kitchen light as if they were sending him a message—one that he would rather not remember. Perhaps it was time to give Otto another history lesson.

"Ah, you found the storage room, I see. Otto, if you decide to go in their again, please let Teresa or me know where you're going. We need to make certain that when you go in there you're safe. By the way, that jacket represents history."

"Like the dead Indian?" Otto asked.

"Sure. Otto, a long time ago, people who lived in the northern part of the United States fought against the people living in the southern states."

"With guns or fists?" Otto asked.

Roger chuckled. "I guess they should have used their fists but, no, they used firearms."

"Why did they fight?"

"Many of those living in the South were using people of color as slaves to work on their farms that they called plantations. The workers didn't have freedom. They didn't have the same rights that the white people had. Abraham Lincoln was the president at that time, and he felt that slavery was wrong. The two sides couldn't come to an agreement, so it finally turned into war. Many people on both sides lost their lives."

"Did you fight in that war?"

"No, Otto. That was a long, long time ago. But, I did participate in some of the reenactments of the Battle of Gettysburg."

"What's an actment?" a bewildered Otto asked.

"Think of it as *pretend*. Remember that time you put on an Easter bunny costume and handed out chocolates to the kids at the day care center?" As Otto nodded his head, Roger went on. "You were just pretending. A reenactment of the Battle of Gettysburg is a pretend version of that event. Shortly after the end of the war, people began to conduct reenactments as a way to remind themselves that a civil war must not ever happen again. Each year, hundreds of people work very hard to create costumes that are exact replicas of what the soldiers on both sides wore when they fought one another. The jacket you have over your arm, Otto, is what a soldier from the North would have worn."

"May I have it?" Otto asked hopefully.

"You may have it. However, I would prefer you only wear it if you participate in a reenactment or some other tribute to the Civil War. Just hang it in your closet so you can look at it often. Think of it as an important collectible—one that represents an important lesson learned."

"Thanks, Roger. I'll take good care of it. I'm glad I wasn't alive during the Civil War 'cause I know I couldn't have hurt anyone just because they lived in the South. Roger, would you ever be able to shoot someone dead?"

"That's a tough question, Otto. One can never say that they would *never* do something. We don't really know what we're capable of doing. If someone would break in here and try to harm you and Teresa, then, yes, I would shoot that person," Roger answered.

Otto, clutching his new possession, hugged Roger. "You are a good man," Otto said as he hurried out the kitchen door.

Roger poured himself another cup of coffee. Seeing that jacket again was doing funny things to his mind. He couldn't erase the scene that was playing over and over in his head. He decided that he would classify what happened, way back then, as his own private war. And, come to think of it, he could do the same with Henry Henderson—but then, Henry was nothing more than a low-down skunk. Otto was right—I am a good man. I take out the garbage.

CHAPTER 28

EVER SINCE THE February STAIRS meeting, Mary Jo had been wrestling with her emotions whenever she would allow herself to think about Ellen or Darius. Mary Jo felt that she was responsible for what happened. Had she not been so focused on what Darius did to her, rather than what he had done to his wife, maybe there would not have been a miscarriage.

As she looked at Cindy, she wanted so badly to share her thoughts with her friend, but shame—pure unadulterated shame—enveloped her. Cindy had warned her, several times, that sometimes these illicit love affairs ended badly. And, there it was—her lover hadn't even tried to reach her for weeks and weeks—a sure sign that it was really over.

"Mary Jo, tell me what's on your mind. You look as if you've seen the devil himself. How may I help you?" Cindy said tenderly.

"God has punished me," Mary Jo said in a whisper. "When I saw Darius, three months ago, I demanded that, no matter what, he had to leave his wife for me. Now, when I think about that, how could I have said that? What gave me the right to demand anything? Look what happened."

"God had nothing to do with the miscarriage. God doesn't punish us that way. You are punishing yourself. Ellen had developed internal problems, and she was unable to support the fetus," Cindy tried to explain.

"Fetus! Say it—it was a child—a baby," Mary Jo cried out.

Mary Jo's outburst had constrained both women into silence. The only sound the two friends could hear was the ticking of the grandfather clock that stood in the hallway. Finally, Cindy said, "Mary Jo, the only way that you're going to straighten out your life is to face your situation head on. Are you ready for that?"

"If I had kept a score card during the affair, it would plainly indicate that I played the part of the fool. Yes, I could blame my conduct on the fact that I had been sexually frustrated for years—but that didn't justify what I did. All that time, both of us were lying to our spouses, never giving any thought to what we were doing to them. And, when I discovered that Darius was telling me lie after lie, I got angry with him," Mary Jo said as she unconsciously twisted her wedding ring.

"Are you going to contact Darius?"

"Probably not. No matter what Darius decides, I have made my decision. I'm going to tell Greg next week when he comes home. I'll be leaving Greg, but not for Darius. I want to be on my own, earn my own living, and try to find the Mary Jo that I really want to be. I'll ask Greg to allow me to tell Beth. I made this mess. Now, I must clean it up. I'm actually looking forward to settling down in a quiet, rather normal routine."

Meanwhile, downtown at the police department, the phone on Detective Fulbright's desk rang. He flipped the switch to speaker, "Fulbright."

"This is Jim Parks, Pittsburgh PD, calling. We found one of your missing persons—Henry Henderson. Some climbers found his body, wrapped in plastic, lying at the bottom of a ravine on Mt. Washington. We got tons of rain the last week or so and that washed away the snow that had probably covered the body for quite some time. The coroner identified him since his name had been stitched on a label on the inside pocket of a leather jacket he was wearing."

⋙ CHAPTER 29 ⋘

MITCH PULLED UP in front of the Cutler County Animal Rescue Association building and jumped out of his truck. Just then he spotted Otto walking Walter and a golden retriever. "Otto, your timing is perfect. Look what I've made for Walter—it's the platform that Walter will stand on to greet the people who go to see David's Dancing Dogs. And, there's also space for you. What do you think?"

"Look, Walter, this is for you. You're going to be a star. Walter has a brand new outfit he'll wear that day. I hope the news people put him on television," said Otto. "Come on, Walter, we must put Billy Boy in the play area before we check out for the day. Don't tell Billy Boy," Otto said as he pointed to the golden retriever, "but tomorrow his new family will be picking him up and taking him to a big home with lots of kids to play with. So, Walter and I wanted to have our last walk with him. We really like him."

"That's nice," Mitch said. When he spotted Mary Jo and Cindy coming out the front door, he smiled broadly. "Hello, Mary Jo. Nice seeing you again, Cindy." Turning directly to Mary Jo, he said, "Here's the platform you requested. I'll make sure that it gets transported on the day of your event. Do you have some time now that we can talk about the Adopt an Animal event for the sanctuary? I thought we might go to my place so you can see the animals to get a better idea of what we may run into with our ideas."

Cindy immediately spoke up, "Go on, Mary Jo. Both Kevin and Lou are in the back. We can take care of things just fine. I know how to close up and the guys will check all the locks."

After Mitch helped Mary Jo into the truck, he handed her a catalog. "Check out the pages I have dog-eared. I thought it might be a good idea to get some of those miniature animals to give out to the kids."

When they arrived at the sanctuary, Mitch said, "There's the ark we can use for the animals. I put in new flooring and gave the whole thing a fresh coat of paint."

"It looks great," Mary Jo said as she walked around the bright yellow and green ark. "I love the colors—it's an attention-getter. And, the hand-carved shamrocks along the sides are absolutely fabulous.

"Of course, the beautiful bird over there is Romeo. He'll need room to strut around and show off his feathers. Next to him, we can put Cleopatra, my adorable little goat. Look, I think she likes you. The Professor, my wise old owl, won't need very much space, but he does like to walk from one perch to another. Depending on the weather, we could put Sir Galahad in an area that we could fence off so the children could pet him. The vet tested him and feels that our tiny horse won't bite anyone. So, that means we can feature four animals," Mitch said as he instinctively took Mary Jo's hand as she was stepping over a small rut. "If we're lucky enough to get the donkeys before the event, we can put them in a fenced off area in the grass."

"We'll need to get pictures of the animals. I can help you design a little certificate to give each child who adopts an animal. You know what I was thinking...we could call this *take an animal friend to lunch.* Their donation of—say five dollars—would get them a certificate with their animal's picture, a little figurine, and a badge that says *I took an animal to lunch.*"

"Mary Jo, you're a genius. Now, it's time for me to take *you* to lunch. Since it's such a beautiful day, I fixed a little picnic lunch. I thought perhaps we could walk down to the river and eat there."

"That sounds lovely."

When they neared his house, Mitch excused himself. "Be right back," he said as he strode to the door.

While she waited for Mitch, Mary Jo had the opportunity to survey the property. It was enchanting. The house, a white-washed stucco affair with a sharply-pitched green roof, looked more like a cottage. A chimney with a decorative cap embraced the short side of the building and Mary Jo wondered if it was in the living room or the kitchen. The window sashes were painted green and each window was hung with yellow shutters that actually worked. Flower boxes, filled with spring pansies and sweet peas, complemented the windows. She could almost picture those boxes in summer, filled with yellow begonias and cascading purple lobelia. A cozy, little porch, tucked under a deep overhang, featured two green rocking chairs with rush seats. It was utterly charming. And, for a moment, Mary Jo wanted to be part of the scene, imagining herself ensconced on a rocking chair, breathing in fragrant viburnums that were just out of eyesight.

She recognized two majestic elm trees that had been strategically planted to provide shade, but allowed ample sunlight to target a small flower garden near the front door. Nearby, in a separate flower bed, a sculpture of St. Francis of Assisi was situated near a whimsical birdfeeder, decorated with Irish harps and Celtic knots. Cardinals and sparrows fought for perches, while two sets of yellow finches availed themselves of the nyjer seed sock, hanging on a nearby shepherd's hook.

Mary Jo could see tidy outbuildings and small fields in the distance. In one enclosure, a pair of black-faced sheep grazed upon the greenest grass she had ever seen. As Mary Jo looked around, she realized that this was one of the most serene sights she had ever encountered in Riverton—so quiet and still. She had lived her entire life in Riverton and never knew this place existed. It was a beautiful secret. God, it was perfect.

When Mitch reappeared, with a wicker basket in hand, his broad smile made him appear even more handsome than ever. The two of them then headed to Timber Run and Mitch's favorite spot. "I made this bench a couple of years ago, so I would always have a place to sit when I wanted to commune with the river. Isn't this the most peaceful spot in the world?"

As Mary Jo looked around, she replied, "You have my vote on that. Now, tell me more about how this sanctuary began."

"My mother had a special talent with animals. People would drop off the abused, the handicapped, the pathetic, and the doomed at her door. Her reputation grew. She also had a green thumb. In the middle of her flower garden she had a statue of St. Francis of Assisi, the patron saint of animals. The statue was a gift from my father, who indulged her in any way he could. We would often find her, sitting on the ground in front of the statue, just admiring her rose bushes. When my dad suggested a bench, she refused. She used to say she really wanted to be as close to her flowers as she could." Mary Jo studied his profile as he stopped and gazed across the river. She hadn't realized how handsome he was.

Mary Jo sensed that he was lost in his memories.

Peacefulness and serenity flowed so easily from him. She wondered if she could ever be at peace with herself as easily as that.

Mitch suddenly realized that he had drifted away. His face turned red. "I apologize. I was lucky. I had a mom and dad, who truly loved one another. They planted my feet firmly on the ground. I hope to do the same thing some day when I marry."

"No need to apologize, Mitch. How wonderful that you have such warm and tender thoughts about your family. That's something to be cherished," Mary Jo said as she patted his hand. "Tell me more about why your parents settled in Pennsylvania."

"My Uncle Martin and my father, Patrick, were born and raised on a farm in the little village of Coolasmuttane, near the town of Charleville in County Cork. Martin, who was much older than my dad, had a fiery personality and a matching temper to boot. He took his politics very seriously and got into a wee bit of a jam with the government and the local garda. My grandparents encouraged him to come to America. He was lucky enough to land in Riverton and find this beautiful property. I guess you could call it the luck of the Irish—to be at the right place at the right time. When he developed heart problems, he asked my dad to come and join him. By this time, my dad was lucky enough to convince my mother to marry him and she came with him. I became a pre-med major, with the idea of going to medical school. However, since money was a real problem, I enlisted in the Army and hoped to qualify for one of their medical programs. Before too long, I found myself in Afghanistan, a sinister, malignant place. I still can't talk too much about that time. I was the only one available to treat our Combat Dogs—everything from cut paws to major wounds. I found it rewarding and comforting."

All was quiet for awhile. As Mitch looked out over the river, he began to shake his head. "Afghanistan changed me. It left scars. I didn't know where to go or what to do. After I left the service, a chance encounter with an old teacher from my high school changed my life. I told him I wanted water and white noise. I wanted peace and quiet. I wanted serenity and stillness. Then, he said, 'Well, why don't you just go home? It's all there—just as you described—and just as you want.' So, I did. And, I began to heal. Through a predictable pattern of farm work, I nourished my soul and eased my nerves by helping the poor and pathetic animals my mother collected."

He wanted to tell her that one day he hoped to share all of this with someone, but he knew he was asking a lot of any woman. He would bide his time.

"I don't have too many nice memories about my brother, though. He didn't feel the same way about the land. You know, my dad brought my mom here as a new bride. I got my love of this place from them. I never understood my brother. We simply didn't get along. He's all about making money. He probably owns half of Singapore by now. However, if I were more like him, I wouldn't have so many financial problems keeping this place open."

"You know, we should investigate the possibility of getting a grant. Let's talk with Darius—" Mary Jo realized what she had just said. "But I'm not sure that he'll be continuing with STAIRS. I know, I'll speak with Greg. He seems to know everyone; especially those with money to give away."

⊰⊱ CHAPTER 30 ⊰⊱

HILDA HENDERSON THOUGHT that she was all cried out. But, as soon as she entered her brother's office, the tears began to flow again. As Detective Fulbright stayed by her side, she had to hold on to the desk to steady herself. She could not bring herself to fully accept that Henry was gone—suffocated, they had told her. But why he was murdered was a question still unanswered.

"Thank you, Detective, for allowing me to recover the picture of George Washington. It means a great deal to me. I truly appreciate your kindness," Hilda said as she yanked out another hanky from her jacket pocket.

Fulbright jumped up on the desk and took the picture off the hook. As he put it face down on the desk, Hilda began to examine it. "Detective, look at this," she said as she pointed to an area where the backing had definitely been disturbed. "It's lumpy there," she said as she pointed to the lower right hand section. Fulbright ran his hand over the spot. "Miss Henderson, you're right. We need to see what's under there. Your brother might have hidden something valuable."

Using his pocket knife, Fulbright gently removed some masking tape. One by one, he then pulled out photographs. "Do you know any of these people?" Fulbright asked. He knew perfectly well who they were, but he wanted to determine how much Hilda might have known about her brother's business dealings, but, she shook her head *no*. "I think we need to remove the paper all around. There could be other items we can't see," Fulbright said.

The only other thing they found was a yellowed, badly-crumpled birth certificate. As Hilda looked at it, she said, "This was for a baby girl by the name of Lilly. I can't make out the last name."

"That document could have been placed in there before you purchased the picture. But, I need to take these with me. They could be a lead," Fulbright said as he carefully gathered the items. His hands shook a bit as he slid the items into evidence bags. He knew that the people in the photos were members of the rich and powerful Fadden family. Could they possibly be mixed up in murder? He realized that he needed to proceed with extreme caution.

CHAPTER 31

OTTO HAD EARNED almost ten dollars this morning helping shop owners along Pine Street. He had to admit that he was feeling a bit tired, so he headed home. As he put his push-broom in his closet, he spotted his new jacket. He loved the brass buttons. He ran his hands over the jacket and said, "Walter, isn't this the most beautiful jacket that you ever did see?" He slipped it on and marched back and forth in front of the mirror. When he took the jacket off, he lovingly smoothed out the wrinkles and hung it back on a padded hanger.

"You know what, Walter. The last time we were in the storage room, I saw a pretty blanket—remember? I think it would look nice on my bed. What do you think? Okay, I agree. Let's go. Oops, wait a minute. I got to tell Teresa where we are going.

The two of them bounded up the stairs, but only Otto went into the kitchen. "Teresa, is it okay to go up to the storage room? I saw a pretty blanket up there. I think it would look nice on my bed," Otto said, crossing his fingers behind him, hoping she would say *yes*.

"Sure, Otto. Don't get into trouble. Remember, keep your eyes on Walter and make sure you turn the light off when you leave."

Otto and Walter quickly disappeared up the front steps

and they were soon sitting on the storage room floor. "Here it is," Otto said. "Look at all the pretty colors," Otto said as he wrapped the blanket around his body.

As he stood up, something fell to the floor. Looking around, he found a framed picture of two men wearing jackets like the one Roger had given him. Otto examined the image carefully. "Walter, I think this one man could be Roger—look," he said as he held the picture in front of Walter. "I don't know who the other man is, but I'm gonna ask Roger."

When the two of them started down the stairs, Otto thought maybe Roger was in his study since he didn't go to the big office every day anymore, so he turned around and walked down the hallway. He put his ear against the door and heard the sound of Roger's shredding machine. Very gently, Otto rapped on the door.

"Come in," he heard Roger say. As Roger spied Otto entering, wrapped up in one of the blankets his mother allowed the children to use when they played *Cowboys and Indians*, he quickly shoved the last pages of his little black book into the shredder and chuckled. "My, my, now, what did you find?"

"I was hoping I could use this on my bed. I really like all the colors," Otto said, once again crossing his fingers.

"Okay, Otto, you don't have to cross your fingers—you may have the blanket. My mother won two blankets at a carnival that she gave to us to use when we played. The kids who wore the blankets were the Indians; the rest of us were cowboys. Now, what do you have in your hand?"

"Is this you, Roger?" Otto asked as he held up the picture.

Roger let out a little gasp. He had forgotten all about the old photo. There he was, a young man, proudly wearing his Union soldier's jacket, standing alongside Erik Danko, his old friend. Finally, he said, "Yes, Otto, I am the one on the right, and a friend of mine, Erik, is on the left. He was my business partner a long, long time ago. While you may have the blanket, I want the picture as a remembrance of Erik. He also has a blanket."

"Is he still your partner?"

Roger sighed. "No. He disappeared one day and I never saw him again."

"Oh, that's sad. Maybe I could be your partner."

"Well, let's see," Roger said as he stroked his beard. "My old partner couldn't keep secrets. Can you keep secrets?"

"Yes, I can. Did your partner disappear 'cause he didn't keep secrets?"

"Sort of. But I'm happy now that I have a new partner. Tell you what…let's make Walter a partner, too. What do you think?"

"Walter will like that. Since he can't talk, we know he'll keep secrets," Otto said as he laughed. "Thank you, Roger," Otto said as he and Walter left the room.

Roger was almost afraid to look at the photo. Those were good times. They were young and ambitious. But, when Erik and he disagreed on business ethics, it all went downhill. He slipped the photo out of the frame and put it into the shredder.

Something unusual was happening to Roger, he was crying.

✦ CHAPTER 32 ✦

WHEN HIS OFFICE door opened and Joshua Fadden walked in, Detective Fulbright jumped up to greet the well-dressed man. "Mr. Fadden, thank you so much for coming. Please have a seat."

"Well, I have never been summoned by the police, so my curiosity is running full-speed. I know I haven't robbed a bank or anything like that. But, I did have a little argument with Greg, though," Joshua said as he smiled broadly.

Fulbright pushed a photo of Henry Henderson across the table. Instantly, Joshua pulled back and his eyes opened wide. "How do you know this man?" asked Fulbright.

"Apparently, you already know that. That bastard had a photo of Morgan Truesdale and me kissing. He demanded money or else he would tell my Uncle Roger. At that time, I was worried about what my uncle might do, so I paid him. However, my uncle has since changed his attitude about Morgan, so all is well between my uncle and me. I only saw that louse two times; once when he showed me the picture, and then when I paid him off. I hope you arrest him," Joshua said almost without taking a breath.

"That would be difficult—he's dead," Fulbright said.

"And you think I might have killed him!" Joshua shouted. "Unbelievable."

"Mr. Fadden, I believe we've found that photo you referred to.

That's why I asked you to come in for an interview. We thought that perhaps you could give us some idea of who could have committed this crime."

For a few minutes, both Joshua and Fulbright were quiet. "Do you have any idea why Henderson would have taken that picture? Did your paths cross at any time before he approached you with the photo and ransom demand?"

"No way," Joshua said sharply. "Before he showed up at my gym that pitiful day, I never knew he existed. And, I have a letter from my uncle that condones my relationship. I can provide you with a copy, if you'd like."

"Did Henderson approach anyone else that you know of?" Fulbright said as he watched Joshua carefully.

Fulbright noticed that Joshua paused a bit longer than necessary before answering. "Your questions are absurd. And, if you're finished with me, I would like to leave. I have a business to run," Joshua said as he stood up.

Fulbright replied, "Mr. Fadden, I'm sorry if I upset you, but we have a murder on our hands. I must question quite a few people to try to get to the bottom of this gruesome killing."

"I accept your apology. If I find out anything that might help you, I'll let you know," Joshua said as he hurried out the door.

When Captain Knoblauch came into Fulbright's office, the detective leaned back in his chair. "Captain, this thing is getting bigger by the minute. Fadden was really upset with me. While he surely doesn't seem capable of murder, he knows more than what he shared with me. The other photos we have of the Faddens are all just head shots, one or more also could have been blackmailed. This is going to be an extremely interesting case."

The captain nodded his head. "Elementary, Sherlock, elementary. Now, get his wife down here."

Joshua heard the laughter as he was leaving the building.

⇜ CHAPTER 33 ⇝

MARY JO HAD decided that this would be the day that she would tell Greg about Darius. Beth's graduation had gone very well and the party they had held for her last evening was fun. When Roger had shown up, Mary Jo almost fainted. Every time she had looked at him last night, it was as if she could hear him reminding her to confess to her husband.

This morning, Beth had left with two of her friends for a back-pack trip in Australia and wouldn't be back for some time. As Cindy had reminded Mary Jo, it would be an ideal time to let Greg know what had happened. As she dressed, she began telling herself that since she was not seeing Darius any more, then perhaps she should just not tell Greg anything. But she also knew that she might not be strong enough to stay away from her lover. However, Roger knows—who knows what *he* will do. During the party, Mary Jo had felt Roger's eyes on her. Whether or not she saw Darius again, she knew that it was only a matter of time before Greg would find out what she had done. Yes, this had to be confession day.

As Greg came down the stairs, she said, "Greg, we need to talk."

"Oh, not this again," he said as he rolled his eyes.

"This is serious. Don't plan on leaving the house until I have had an opportunity to tell you something very important," Mary Jo said firmly.

"Alright," Greg replied in a voice that indicated he was annoyed. "What's so damned important?"

As soon as Greg sat down, Mary Jo sat across from him, took a deep breath, and said, "I've been unfaithful."

Greg stared at her. "Say what?"

"I had an affair for more than eight months. However, I have ended it." She paused and then added, "I'm not looking for forgiveness."

Greg was silent. He blinked his eyes several times. "And who was the lucky man?" he asked sarcastically.

"Darius Davis—the man who is helping the animal shelter prepare for STAIRS."

"Well, it looks like Mr. Davis helped himself to a bit more than he should have."

"I have ended it with him. I want to live on my own. I'm asking you to allow me to tell Beth. I owe it to her to tell her the truth," Mary Jo said nervously.

"Oh, don't you think you owe her more than that? You go around, humping other men, and now you're worried what she'll think about you? Isn't that a bit self-righteous—even for a whore?"

"Greg, look, we can—"

"No. Now it's my turn to talk. You have some nerve. I work my ass off making a good life for you and Beth, while you're running all over town playing hide the weeny with some joker. You're not getting this house—not now—not ever. I'll fight your every move to share my money—I made it—not you. Roger was right all along—you're not worth the room you take up. I'll give you one week to get your things packed and get out of here. Meanwhile, I'll stay at the hotel since I don't want to see your face again. Oh, and you better not take anything from this house that's not yours. Whores really don't need much since they have a unique way of paying for what they want."

About an hour later, when Greg left the house, carrying two suitcases, Mary Jo was still sitting in the living room. There were no tears, but the pain she felt was devastating—much worse than what she had expected.

CHAPTER 34

W HEN CRYSTAL RECEIVED a call from Detective Fulbright, asking her to report to the station, her heart sank. She had been worrying ever since she spotted the newspaper picture of her blackmailer as a missing person. But that was months ago. How she was going to face a detective, Crystal had no idea. Her stomach was in knots, and she couldn't stop weeping. She couldn't afford to let the world know what she had done, especially now that she had Sinclair interested. She had only been a teenager at the time of that stupid accident and felt that she had been unfairly judged. She hadn't *meant* for anyone to die. It had been an accident. It wasn't her fault. Remembering those death threats she had received made her knees shake. Perhaps she should call a lawyer. Or, maybe she should just lie.

These thoughts were proving to be too much for her to handle, so she blocked them out by thinking about what she should wear. She decided to remove some of her jewelry— don't look too wealthy, she told herself. Choosing a plain black pencil skirt and a demure white blouse, she hurriedly dressed. She tried to picture what this Fulbright guy would look like— probably obese and unshaven. After all, Riverton wasn't a major city, so perhaps he also wasn't too smart.

As she mounted the half dozen steps in front of the precinct, Crystal was trying to reassure herself that she had nothing to worry about. She didn't fail to notice that she was drawing a great deal of attention from the officers that were stationed at the front desk. Perhaps, just perhaps, she would have the same effect on Fulbright.

One of the officers almost fell over himself getting up to greet her. She turned on her brightest smile and said, "I'm Mrs. Joshua Fadden and I'm here to see Detective Fulbright."

"Right this way, Mrs. Fadden. Isn't it nice that the sun is shining brightly today, particularly after all those days of rain that we have experienced?" the desk clerk gushed.

"Well, I find rain very soothing. However, I have to agree that there is such a thing as too much of a good thing," Crystal purred as the officer opened Fulbright's office door.

Fulbright was up on his feet almost instantly. "Mrs. Fadden, thank you very much for coming in. I'll try not to keep you too long."

When she realized that Fulbright was a handsome man, Crystal made certain that she showed off her legs as she positioned herself in a chair next to his paper-loaded desk. "I can't imagine why I'm here."

Fulbright slid Henry's photo across the desk. "Do you know this man?"

Crystal certainly recognized her blackmailer. She kept staring at the photo to avoid having eye contact with Fulbright and to gain a little time. She took several seconds before she said, "He does look familiar, but I can't say that I do. I go to so many charity events with Senator Althouse that I simply can't remember the names of those I interact with. Sorry." Crystal had clasped her hands together to keep them from shaking.

"Did this man ever approach you with a business deal?"

Crystal put her hand over her mouth to feign complete

surprise. "My goodness, no! For what reason?" she asked as she shook her head.

"He could have had blackmail in mind," Fulbright said as he observed her reaction.

Crystal forced a slight giggle. "My goodness, Detective, blackmail—are you serious?"

"We found a few photos in his office and yours was among them. And, since Henderson was a rather shady fellow, we're looking into the possibility that he may have found something *personal* that he decided was worth some money for him. Did anything happen in your family that would fall into that category?"

"Well, I do have an idea. You see, my husband left me—not for another woman—but for a man. When Uncle Roger found out about his double life, he encouraged him to make it right with his lover. That couldn't be a reason for blackmail, though, since his uncle accepted his lifestyle. But I can't speak for my sister-in-law. We don't communicate with one another."

"Thank you for sharing that with me. You see, this man met with an unfortunate death."

"Detective Fulbright, you don't mean that you thought I might be involved in murder? Heavens, while I'll miss Joshua, I've realized for some time what his proclivity was. We parted as friends, and I wouldn't have a reason to commit a crime. Really, I'm shocked!"

"Mrs. Fadden, this is normal procedure. I must admit, nonetheless, that it has to be difficult for ladies of refinement," Fulbright said gently.

"I intend to tell Sinclair Hancock about this interview. You know, he and I will be attending The Policemen's Ball next month. In fact, he's purchased an entire table. I'm certain that he won't be pleased that I had to sit through this afront," Crystal said, obviously annoyed.

Fulbright's mind was racing. As if it weren't bad enough that this case involved the wealthy Faddens, now it had spilled over to one of the wealthiest men in the Commonwealth. Sinclair Hancock could buy and sell the kit-and-caboodle of Faddens. "Of course, I understand. A woman of your stature, with a pristine reputation like yours, would naturally be offended. But, please remember, the interview was only a matter of procedure."

"I trust I may leave now?"

"Certainly, Mrs. Fadden. I hope to see you at the Ball," Fulbright said as he opened the door.

Fulbright sauntered down the hallway to the captain's office. "Hell, in no time at all, she threw her husband and her sister-in-law under the bus. She's good. I'll bet you a month's pay that Henderson blackmailed her."

"You know, I'm not a betting man, but if the hair on the back of your neck stood up, then she's guilty," the captain said.

"She'd never wrap a body in plastic, but she has the money to pay someone else to do it for her. Tomorrow, I'll call her sister-in-law and invite her down for an interview. I wonder what secrets she's keeping. Then I'll tackle Greg Fadden."

"Hell, don't forget the boss of the family, Roger Fadden."

"I thought I'd save him for last. One of them might go running to him for help. His picture wasn't included in those that Hendersen had hidden, but, who knows, he may be just as guilty as the rest of them. This case can't get any stranger," Fulbright said assuredly.

The captain smiled and replied, "Don't bet on that!"

CHAPTER 35

OTTO HEARD THE distant sound of thunder and tried to go back to sleep. However, as the sound was getting progressively louder, he tried putting his head under the pillow. As he reached for his covers, he realized that Walter was pulling them off. "Walter, what's wrong with you? It's only a thunderstorm. It won't hurt you." Walter persisted. "It's too early for breakfast," Otto pleaded. Walter kept it up until he had all the covers on the floor. Otto finally gave up and sat up in bed. "Alright, Walter, you win. I'll get up," Otto said as he rubbed his eyes.

While Otto was getting dressed, Walter continued to scratch at the door and whine. "My goodness, Walter, I'm hurrying as fast as I can. I've never seen you act like this. What's wrong?"

Since Roger had given strict orders that Walter was not allowed in the kitchen their usual routine was that Walter would follow Otto up the stairs to the kitchen, and lie down by the doorway. Much to Otto's surprise, however, Walter had worked his way in front of Otto, ran up the stairs and hurried into the kitchen.

"No, Walter, no. You know that you're not—" Otto's eyes opened wide when he saw that Roger was lying on the floor with his arms outstretched. Just then, a bolt of lightning lit up the entire kitchen and Walter began whining louder. Otto tiptoed over to Roger, leaned down, and touched his cold face. "Oh, Walter, you were trying to tell me...you were trying to tell me...I'm sorry, Roger, I didn't know you needed me." As Otto sat beside Roger, the rain began pounding against the windows harder than Otto had ever heard before.

Just then Otto heard the sound of Teresa's battered, old station-wagon pulling into the driveway. Otto opened the side door just a crack and called out, "Hurry, Teresa, something's wrong with Roger. He's on the floor and isn't moving."

Teresa slammed her car door and ran up the sidewalk. She pulled her hood over her head and bolted up the steps like a jack-rabbit just as another bolt of lightning whipped overhead. She hurried past Otto and dropped to her knees alongside Roger. She didn't feel a pulse, but noticed he was cold to the touch. Rummaging in her large canvas handbag, she pulled out her cell phone and dialed 911. While Otto sat beside Roger with Walter on his lap, Teresa called Greg and Joshua.

"Roger, Roger," Otto cried. "My partner. I love you. I promise I will keep our secrets—all of them. I won't be like Erik. I won't disappear." Then Otto collapsed in a heap on the floor.

By the time the rain had subsided a bit, the police, the EMT's, and the coroner arrived almost simultaneously. Joshua, Greg, and Mary Jo weren't too far behind. Mary Jo rushed over to Otto and guided him into the living room. She wanted to console him and prevent him from seeing the removal of Roger's body from the house.

Otto hugged Walter and whispered to him, "I'm not sure how, but Roger will be going to heaven. I wish we could go with him."

Greg decided that he would be the one to go along with

Roger and take care of the finalities. He called Mary Jo over and said, "Would you be willing to stay here at Roger's home for a while? While I know Roger took care of many aspects of his estate, it'll take some time to get things straightened out—you know, we just can't move Otto out."

"Of course, I'll stay. I'll help in any way. Do you want me to take care of the household help? We should keep them on for some time to make it less upsetting for them."

Joshua squinted his eyes. "Guys, is there something I don't know?"

Mary Jo and Greg looked at one another. Finally, Greg said, "Mary Jo and I are divorcing. Since she was going to get her own place, she can stay here until she finds a suitable place."

Joshua was surprised. "I'm sorry. I hope things work out for the two of you."

"Thanks," Greg said. I don't know if I'll be back here later, Mary Jo. If you need help getting some of your personal effects moved here, give me a holler," Greg said as he hopped into the ambulance.

Joshua turned to Mary Jo and said, "It seems that there's a new dawn on the horizon. Look, the sun is shining brightly now and Roger's river is calm and serene. Roger accomplished many goals in his business life, but I always felt that he was really a lonely man. The rest of us Faddens must now take over the reins and keep his legacy alive."

⮞ CHAPTER 36 ⮜

W HEN DETECTIVE FULBRIGHT heard about Roger Fadden's death on the radio, he swore a blue streak because the Henderson case had become more muddled. While the murder of Henry Henderson was technically under the jurisdiction of Jim Parks at the Pittsburgh Police Department, Fulbright has a vested interest in the case. "No way," Fulbright muttered as he stormed out his front door.

The first thing a testy Fulbright did when he arrived at work was to call Jim Parks. However, Parks wasn't in his office and that irked Fulbright even more. When the two of them had talked yesterday, Parks indicated that he had issued an APB for someone named Horse, a low-life, who had a penchant for using plastic in unique ways. Fulbright was eager to hear if Parks had found the guy.

To add to his irritation, he realized he couldn't call Mary Jo Fadden to come in for an interview like he had planned to do, until after old mam Fadden had been buried. The only thing he could hope for now was for Parks to grab his perp and arrest him. Then, maybe things would calm down. When his phone rang, it startled him enough to knock his phone off the hook. "Fulbright," he yelled loudly.

"Holy hell, Fulbright," Parks said, "is that anger aimed at me?"

"Sorry, Parks, but old man Fadden died this morning, and I'm upset that I didn't get to talk with him. How did you make out with your perp?"

"Get ready for more bad news. We traced an RV that Horse had owned to a little town called Hobbs in New Mexico. However, Horse had traded the RV in for an old Ford Galaxy and some cash. Before we could issue another APB, in the middle of the freaking desert—mind you—the freaking desert—the Galaxy blew up. There was another body in the damned car, but they haven't ID'd it yet. They're still sifting through the rubble, but they don't hold out much hope since the whole damned car is now in a zillion little pieces."

"Now what?"

"Well, we need to know why Henderson was in Pittsburgh— did he come here on his own, or did someone send him here? We suspect that Horse was skimming money off the top and perhaps his gang caught on. Now, it's also possible that someone in Riverton might have been involved. My guess is that this person would have been much higher up the ladder than Henderson. At this time, what's your take on the two Faddens that you've interviewed?"

"Joshua claimed that his uncle encouraged him to leave his wife and marry his lover. His proof was a handwritten note that his uncle had given him on Christmas. However, a murder could have been arranged before Christmas. Now, as far as Crystal is concerned, *no* to actually committing a murder, but *yes,* she could be involved in plotting one," Fulbright explained. "I do think this one would do almost anything for money."

"I know it's my crime to solve, but I sure could use some help," Parks responded. "I appreciate the interviews you've already conducted, but keep me posted on the two remaining ones," Parks urged. "When we solve this, I'll treat you to a Steelers game next season. That is, if nothing else blows the hell up, or no one else croaks in the meantime."

"Sounds good to me. I plan to attend Fadden's memorial. Who knows what I might find there. Call you later," Fulbright said as he opened Henderson's file folder one more time.

⇜ CHAPTER 37 ⇝

S EVERAL DAYS BEFORE, while feeding his animals, Mitch had heard about Roger Fadden's death on the radio. He hadn't been sure if he should contact Mary Jo, or what he could do for her at this time. He thought that perhaps it would be better just to send flowers or a card. Mitch wasn't too familiar with social graces and such things. He realized that if things were different—really different—he would gather her in his arms and hold her for a long time.

Today, he would be attending Fadden's memorial—that's the least he could do. The obituary notice indicated that Fadden was to be cremated, and that, in lieu of flowers, contributions could be made to the Church of Joyous Tidings. He couldn't get used to the idea that everyone he had talked to about Roger thought the man was almost a saint. On the other hand, he didn't have any proof that he wasn't. After all, Mitch had never even met the man, but his instinct, which seldom let him down, made him feel otherwise.

Mitch took the end seat in the last row of pews. He noticed that Otto was sitting in the front row with the Faddens. The pews in the church filled rapidly. Mitch spotted several members of the STAIRS committee, but otherwise he didn't know anyone around him. The ushers were busy setting up folding chairs in the activity room for the overflow. When

Mitch saw Mary Jo, his heart fluttered a bit. She was wearing a black suit and a small veiled hat that only partially covered her curly hair.

Suddenly, Mitch had a sense that something important was happening. Greg Fadden was escorting a well-dressed, elderly woman down the center aisle to a seat in the second row. Mitch heard a woman near him whisper to her friend, "That's Sarah Hamilton McIntyre." Heads turned as people tried to get a glimpse of the very wealthy woman.

Morgan Truesdale stood up, approached Mrs. McIntyre, and spoke to her briefly. He then sat down on the bench that was in front of a Steinway that Mrs. McIntyre had provided for the memorial. The strains of *Clair de Lune* filled the air. No one spoke or made any noise. Everyone seemed to be enchanted by the music.

Just then, Mitch got a glimpse of Walter, with his crooked tail, heading down the center aisle, dragging a leash behind him. His first instinct was to grab the leash and pull him back, but the scene so enchanted him that he let the dog alone. Walter stopped alongside Otto and nudged him on his arm. Otto's face lit up. He leaned over and scooped Walter up in his arms. Otto whispered into Walter's ear, "You got loose. You wanted to say goodbye to Roger, too. Oh, you wonderful dog. Roger and I both love you."

The minister moved to the lectern, smiled, and then said, "It seems we almost forgot someone—welcome Walter. Our Lord works in mysterious ways," he said to a smiling audience. The minister then gave a short eulogy, expounding on the many contributions that Roger had made to the church and its members. He also mentioned that Roger had provided the funding necessary for the expenses involved in the opening day's ceremonies for STAIRS. Mitch shifted uneasily in his seat. No matter, he thought, I still don't like him. Anxiously, he looked around. Would it be possible for God to strike him dead for feeling this way about someone whose ashes were in a silver urn that was resting near the lectern?

Joshua then stood up and walked to the pulpit. He shared some of his favorite memories of his Uncle Roger. Mitch hadn't known that Roger had raised the boys after their parents were killed in an accident. Now, he was sounding like a good guy—Mitch was ready to change his mind about the Dearly Departed. Greg was the next one to speak. He gave his uncle accolades, too. He also told some funny stories that made the mourners smile. He thanked Mrs. McIntyre for providing the Steinway and Morgan for allowing everyone to hear such beautiful music. Greg paused a few seconds, gazed at his relatives, and said, "None of us could deny that he always put family first. Our greatest gift to Roger would be to emulate his love, concern and loyalty for family."

When Morgan started playing the introduction to the hymn, *This is My Father's Home,* the choir stood up and joined in. As the sun streamed through the stained-glass windows, something almost magical happened to Mitch—the bitterness he had felt in his heart dissipated. Roger Fadden could not have had a more devout memorial if he had planned it himself.

When the service was over and people began to move to the dining area for the luncheon, Mitch slipped out the side door. He knew that he didn't want to see Mary Jo with Greg. He wondered if he would be punished for even thinking about another man's wife when he had just felt closer to his religious beliefs than he had in a long time. As he climbed into his truck, Mitch had no idea that he was being followed by Detective Fulbright.

CHAPTER 38

MITCH WASN'T SURE what to do about the STAIRS meeting that was being held today. So, he took a chance and drove to the animal shelter to see if Mary Jo was there. When he pulled into the parking lot, he smiled when he spotted her car.

As he opened the door, Mary Jo said, "Good morning, Mitch. Nice to see you again."

"Hi, there," Cindy said as she watched Mitch, who was trying to act nonchalant.

"I was pleased to see you at the memorial service. How nice of you," Mary Jo said.

"Morning," Mitch said as he felt his face turn red. "I thought we could go to the meeting together. But, with the memorial and such, I wasn't sure what your plans were. Maybe we could have lunch."

"Cindy, would you take over the counter for a few minutes? I need to speak with Mitch in my office," Mary Jo said a little hesitantly.

"Sure," Cindy said as she gave Mary Jo a knowing look.

When Mary Jo and Mitch were seated in her office, Mitch said, "Are you okay?"

Mary Jo smiled. "Yes, Mitch, I'm fine. I need to bring you up to date on what has happened in my life. Greg and I have separated," she said softly. "I'll be staying at Roger's home for a while—at least until things get straightened out."

"Mary Jo you don't have to..."

"Wait—there's more. Oh, this part is hard," Mary Jo said as she closed her eyes. "I was unfaithful. I had an affair for several months. I broke if off..." Mary Jo became quiet and Mitch was dumbfounded.

"Mary Jo, you don't have to tell me any of this," Mitch said gently.

"Yes, I do. You see, my affair was with Darius Davis."

Mitch swallowed hard. He had sensed all along that they were close—he was right. It still did not change how he felt about Mary Jo, but he knew that this wasn't the time to tell her that. "I understand."

"I'm not sure you do, but I don't expect you to. I don't understand it myself. I can't tell you why it happened. But, I can tell you that the affair is over. Now I must work on getting the *Mary-Jo-I-want-to-be* back and functioning. But it was only fair to let you know all of this since he may still be working with us on STAIRS. However, if you want to drop out of our plans, I'll understand."

"I won't be dropping out. I want to help you with your plans, and I hope you'll still want to help me with mine. Mary Jo, I want to spend time with you. I want to be around you. I promise I won't put any pressure on you," Mitch said as he took Mary Jo's hands in his. "If friendship is all you and I ever have, I'll accept that. But please don't walk out of my life." There—he had promised himself that he wouldn't share his feelings—especially after her confession, but he had to let her know that he valued her. What happened in her past didn't affect him. He desperately wanted her companionship. As he looked at Mary Jo, he thought of an incident that had happened many years before. He had found a little kitten, who had been badly mangled and he wanted to make it well. His mom had told him that he would only win the game if he was slow and gentle and let the kitten tell him when she was well. Mary Jo had been mangled and had lost her way for awhile. He would wait and let her tell him when she was ready to be loved again.

Mary Jo was astounded. No one had ever said such lovely words to her. His sincerity and honesty touched her deeply. She knew that she certainly wasn't ready to begin a new relationship, but she really wanted to keep Mitch as a dear friend. "Mitch, that was beautiful. Now, if you still want to go to the STAIRS meeting, I'm ready," she said tenderly.

"My mother had a favorite Irish proverb: *True friendship is like one soul living in two bodies.* You bet I'm ready for the meeting," he said as he rushed to open the door for her.

As they neared the meeting place, Mitch began to worry about whether or not Darius Davis would show up. His first thought was that he should knock the jerk on his ass. Now was the time that Mitch wished he had a beautiful white stallion—he could pick up Mary Jo, put her next to him, and ride into the sunset—isn't that how it goes in fairy tales?

"If Darius comes to the meeting, Mary Jo, I want you to know that I will behave myself as much as I would like to tell him off. If you want to speak to him in private, I totally understand."

"I really doubt that he'll show up. If he does, I plan to behave myself, too," she said as she smiled weakly.

Since opening day for STAIRS was less than two weeks away, the committee had a full agenda. Just as the gavel was wrapped, a woman came running into the room. "Excuse me, I'm Gloria Winters, and I'm representing Davis Media today."

Mary Jo stood up. "Over here, Gloria," Mary Jo said as she pulled another chair to the table. The only thing going through Mary Jo's mind at that moment was that Darius didn't even have the courtesy to call her, or have someone in his company contact her so that she could have given the woman a decent welcome. When the committee took a coffee break, Mary Jo introduced Mitch and herself and the two of them shared what activities were planned for the four-day event.

"I'm sorry that I wasn't able to talk with you before today, but I just got this assignment this morning. So, please clue me in on what you'll need Davis Media to do for you. Things have been chaotic lately at the office with the problems the boss's wife has been having. It's been difficult getting back to normal," Gloria said as she skimmed the agenda.

"Ah, normal...I guess we all wish for that," Mary Jo replied. I won't need your help with David's Dogs since the venue has access to all he needs. However, Mitch needs help with the program he'll hold in the park. While we have permission to park the ark alongside the ball field, we must set up and break down the same day. Is that going to be a problem?"

"No. I'd really like to see the space and the ark, though. That will give me the information I'll need to prepare the technicians. Could we do that now?"

"Sure. I'll be happy to drive you over. When we're finished, I'll bring you back here for your car," Mitch offered. "First, however, I have a surprise. Tomorrow morning, I expect to receive the delivery of twin baby donkeys!"

"Oh, Mitch, how wonderful. Oh, oh, I just thought of something. Let's have a contest to give them names. The children will simply love that. They can fill out an entry slip and, at the end of the program, you can pull the winning slip and that will tell us what their names will be. I can't wait to see them," Mary Jo said as she gave Mitch a hug.

"Okay, ladies, let's get going." Mitch, who could still feel the warmth of Mary Jo's arms around his shoulders, silently congratulated himself for getting such a marvelous *thank you*. Maybe that one was just the beginning.

CHAPTER 39

"MRS. FADDEN, FIRST let me offer my condolences on the loss of your father-in-law. Also, I appreciate that you were willing to come in for an interview," Detective Fulbright said earnestly.

"Thank you, Detective Fulbright. However, I'm at a loss regarding the purpose of the interview," Mary Jo replied.

As he pushed Henry Henderson's picture across his desk, he asked, "Do you know this man?"

"Wasn't his picture in the papers as a missing person?" Mary Jo asked.

"Yes. Do you know him?"

"No, I don't. What do I have to do with this man?" a perturbed Mary Jo asked.

"This man was murdered in Pittsburgh. When we examined his office, we found your photo among several others that had been hidden. Did he ever approach you in a blackmail shakedown?"

Mary Jo heaved a sigh. "Really, you've got to be kidding. I told you I never met him. Why he had a photo of me, I really don't know."

"I don't mean to upset you, but we believe that he intended to blackmail several of you Faddens. Is there any reason that he knew something about you that he felt would be bait for blackmail?" Fulbright asked as he kept a close eye on her.

She could feel her nervousness growing and she didn't want to tell him about Darius. Fulbright interrupted her thoughts when he blurted out, "Are there any problems in your marriage?"

A frustrated Mary Jo turned to face Fulbright and said, "Yes. It appears that you know that my husband and I have separated."

"I must ask: Is a third party involved?"

"I'm not sure that you have the right to ask me such a personal question, Detective."

"We're dealing with a man's murder, Mrs. Fadden. I'm not a reporter looking for a scandalous story," Fulbright said as he leaned in a little closer to Mary Jo. "I'm trying to determine what Henderson was up to, and whether there's a connection between the Faddens and him."

"Does this mean you have photos of some of the other family members, too?"

"Yes."

Mary Jo closed her eyes. The only sound that could be heard was the ticking of the old-fashioned clock that hung on the wall of the small room. "I was involved with a married man. We no longer see one another. But, I told my husband—he knows everything."

"Before Christmas or after?"

"What?"

"Did you tell him before Christmas or after?" Fulbright emphasized.

Instantly, she remembered Roger's Christmas letters. "After," she stated. "Why is that important?"

"I can't tell you that. Who was the married man?"

"Detective, you have no right to ask me that. I told you the affair is over."

"Henderson might have approached him, too. I really need to know who it was. Mrs. Fadden, murder is a crime—one that we are expected to solve no matter who's involved," Fulbright said pointedly.

"Alright—Darius Davis of Davis Media. Can you tell me which family members you have interviewed so far?"

"I can't tell you that, either. But, you're certainly free to ask them."

⇌ CHAPTER 40 ⇋

G REG PULLED HIS car behind Mary Jo's as the two of them drove into the wide, oval driveway in front of Roger's home. "Mary Jo, just take the small things and put them at the bottom of the stairs. I'll get the rest and I'll take everything upstairs for you. Which bedroom are you going to use?"

"The one at the end of the hallway, next to the storage room," she replied as she took several shoeboxes out of the trunk of her car and hurried in the front door. When she noticed that Teresa was taking inventory of the items in the large china closet, Mary Jo said over her shoulder, "Greg, I'm going to help Teresa."

Greg carried all the clothes Mary Jo had on hangers up the steps. As he passed by the storage room, he spotted Otto sitting on the floor, setting up train tracks, while Walter was close by. "Hi, Otto. I used to play with that train when I was a boy." He leaned over and gave Walter a belly rub.

"Is it okay if I run it?" Otto asked hopefully. "Teresa said it was okay, but if it's your train, I should have asked you."

"No, it's not mine. You go right ahead. If you have any problems with the engine, let Teresa know and we can get it fixed. Since they haven't been played with for so long, they may need some attention."

"Thank you, Mr. Greg," Otto said happily, as he put on an engineer hat that he had found in the bottom of a trunk.

When Greg rejoined Mary Jo, he said, "I've got to run. I have an appointment with a Detective Fulbright at police headquarters."

Mary Jo almost dropped the cup of coffee she was holding. She motioned for him to go out into the hallway with her. Very quietly, she said, "Wait a minute. I just saw him yesterday. He's investigating the murder of someone named Henry Henderson."

"Henderson? I don't know anyone with that name. Why us?"

"Apparently, our photos were found hidden somewhere in Henderson's office, and the cops figure that he may have had plans to blackmail us," Mary Jo said almost in a whisper.

"Do you think that he knows about your..."

"I told the detective about the affair and that I confessed to you. He wanted to know if you were aware of the affair before or after Christmas. I immediately connected that to Roger's Christmas letters. Oh, Greg, look what I have caused; I'm so sorry," Mary Jo said quietly.

"Isn't it a little late to apologize for ripping my family apart? I hope your Adonis was worth it," Greg said, emphasizing every word.

"Look, I'm staying here as a favor to you and your brother. If you don't stop berating me, I'll leave. I was the one who did wrong. I can't undo it. So, it's up to you—we keep this arrangement peacefully or not at all," Mary Jo said as she crossed her arms.

Greg paused. "Do you know if they questioned Joshua or Crystal?"

"He wouldn't say."

"What about him?"

"Him?"

"Davis," Greg replied sharply.

"I don't know," Mary Jo replied just as sharply.

"Mary Jo, you may have to stay here for several months. Trying to settle Roger's estate may get messy before it gets any better. If that poses a problem for you, we'll have to come up with a different plan. Look, we're not involved in any murder. I'll put an end to this ridiculous invasion into our private lives. Leave it to me." Greg walked back into the dining room where Teresa was and said, "If you need more help in going through the china and the curios, give me a call."

Mary Jo called after him and said, "Do we have a deal?"

As he headed for his car, he turned and looked at her for a few long seconds and replied, "Yeah."

After Mary Jo and Teresa had been working for a while, Teresa said, "I better get lunch ready. Otto's probably starved by now. My, oh my, how that man loves to eat. Will a grilled cheese sandwich and some tomato soup be okay with you?"

"Sounds great. I'll go up and get Otto."

She could hear the toy train running as she climbed the stairs. When the train's little whistle blew, Walter barked. "Otto, its lunch time."

"Hello, Mary Jo. Look. Greg wasn't sure the train would run—but it works okay." Otto turned the engine off. "Mary Jo, I've been wondering. When someone tells you a secret, does that mean you can't tell anyone else?"

"You mean like the dead Indian?" Mary Jo said lightheartedly.

"Yeah, and other things," Otto said as he stood up. "Can people in heaven see what we do and hear what we say? I don't want to disappoint Roger."

"I'd like to think that they watch over us. I do know one

thing for certain, Otto. Roger liked you and considered you a friend," Mary Jo said as she led the way down the stairs.

After they finished their lunch, Otto said, "Mary Jo, if I know where Roger hid something, but I can't read what it says, would it be okay for me to tell you where it is?"

Mary Jo could tell that Otto had been agonizing over this, so she said, "Tell you what, Otto. It's okay to tell me. If it turns out to be something important, I'll tell you."

Otto jumped up and said, "Good, you must come with me."

Mary Jo was surprised when he stopped at Roger's home study. "But, Otto, the only thing in there is Roger's old desk."

"That's where the secret is," Otto whispered convincingly.

"Joshua went through the desk and took out all the paperwork before they moved it here," Mary Jo argued.

"But he didn't touch the Indian," Otto argued back.

Mary Jo rolled her eyes. "Okay, Otto, show me."

Otto scurried over to the desk. "Come back here," Otto directed Mary Jo. "Look down there," Otto said as he pointed to what Mary Jo thought was probably the head of an Indian with a headdress. "Now, watch," Otto instructed. He pressed on the carving and, to Mary Jo's surprise, a small drawer silently opened. "See!" Otto said proudly. Mary Jo remembered Otto's story that a dead Indian was buried in the back lawn, and now, by pressing on the nose of the carving on the front drawer, she discovered a small pile of index cards with strange markings. Chills went up Mary Jo's spine. An ominous feeling overcame her.

Mary Jo sat down on the floor. She immediately pulled off the rubber band that was around one of the sets of index cards. She felt queasy as she looked at names of cities and countries and what appeared to be large figures of money. One small envelope had the word *Horse* written on it. And, in parentheses, the name *Erik*. Mary Jo recalled that a long time ago, Roger had had a partner with that name. The feeling of dread was stronger. She needed to get a closer look at the index cards before she could make a decision regarding what to do with these *secrets*.

"Otto, I need to take these items along with me. You see, the lawyers, who are taking care of Roger's possessions, will need them. I want to thank you for letting me know about these papers—Roger would be proud of you. You must not tell anyone else what we found. Roger wouldn't want others to know about the secret drawer, either."

Mary Jo felt guilty. Ironically, the items she was holding might destroy Roger Fadden's pristine reputation all together. She should turn all of this over to Greg. After all, he was in charge of Roger's estate. However, he had been so nasty she really didn't want to deal with him again. She knew that she had to study these cards before she would do anything with them. Suddenly, it dawned on her that all of this might negatively impact Beth. *That* she would not allow.

CHAPTER 41

G REG WAS REALLY irritated. He was angry at himself. He was infuriated with Mary Jo. He had thought his world was perfect, and then, piece by piece, it fell apart. First, he just had a go-around with Mary Jo after he had repeatedly told himself that that wasn't going to happen. He had never suspected anything about the affair even though it had lasted quite a few months. How stupid he must be. And, it was asinine that anyone could suspect him of murder. He stomped up the steps in front of the Police Department and grabbed the door rail. By now, he could feel the anger all over his body.

"Good day, sir, how may I help you?" a female officer asked.

"Greg Fadden to see Detective Fulbright."

"Right this way," the officer said as she ushered him down the hall. "First door on your right."

As he stood in front of Fulbright's office, he heaved a big sigh. He intended to take control of this so-called interview from the start. He wasn't going to have some two-bit cop even suggest that he, Greg Fadden, was under suspicion.

As soon as Greg stepped in his office, Fulbright stood up and put out his hand. "Mr. Fadden, thank you so much for coming in."

Ignoring the outstretched hand, Greg said harshly, "Fulbright, I want you to know that I'm much too busy for this nonsense. I just lost my uncle, I have lawyers calling me night and day, and my wife and I have separated. Now, you have some trumped-up excuse to question me about a guy that I don't even know, was murdered and you consider me a suspect."

"I assure you, Mr. Fadden, we're only following normal procedures. You probably also know that this man had photos of you and your wife in his office. Since the victim was a low-life, we thought that he might have been blackmailing one or both of you," Fulbright said. He carefully watched Greg as he slid Henderson's photo across his desk.

"No use showing me his damned photo. I don't know the man; I'm a highly respected businessman and I don't associate with scum. My family and I are in mourning. Have you no conscience?" Greg asked.

"We try our best to solve all crimes, regardless of the character or station of the victim. Are you saying that you don't know Henry Henderson and that he never approached you with any scheme?" Fulbright explained.

"Yes! I don't know why he had our photos. So, I'd appreciate it if you'd stop harassing my family."

"Did your Uncle Roger ever mention the name Henry Henderson or indicate that he needed the services of a private detective?" Fulbright asked.

"No. Absolutely not."

"Mr. Fadden, does your company have any branch offices in Pittsburgh?" Fulbright asked as he looked over his notes.

"What the hell does that have to do with this circus?" And, with that, Greg got up and stormed out of Fulbright's office. He more than earned the inheritance that he'd be receiving before too long. If Roger had anything to do with that dead body they found in Pittsburgh, all Greg knew was that he was not going to let that get in *his* way.

Fulbright was surprised that Greg Fadden had conducted himself in such a defensive manner. Oh, how he hoped that he would be able to pin Henderson's murder on that big-feeling SOB. No wonder his wife left him. He was disappointed that he had been unable to get any usable information from the Faddens. While he had planned on interviewing Roger's personal secretary, he was shocked when he discovered that he never had one. Apparently, when Roger needed secretarial work, he simply used a member from the stenographic pool, or he spoke into a recorder. When Fulbright learned this, he felt like this might be a case that he would never solve.

CHAPTER 42

Mary Jo was up half the night looking at the paperwork she had found in Roger's secret desk drawer. She couldn't understand why Roger felt the need to hide the papers and the index cards. If they were harmful, he would have destroyed them. Then, it suddenly occurred to her that he had probably planned to do just that, but fate had intervened. While it wouldn't surprise her at all to discover that Roger had been involved in some money-making scheme, she still could not imagine that he would be involved in a murder.

If she turned everything over to Detective Fulbright, it could very well destroy both Greg and Joshua—she couldn't fathom hurting them. After all, she had been a member of the Fadden family for a quarter of a century. Then, there was Beth—her precious, innocent child. She might very well be the head of the Fadden family in the future. While Roger didn't want Greg to marry Mary Jo, he had tolerated her. However, he dearly loved Beth and she deserved a chance to spread her wings and prove herself in her own time.

Roger's will could take months to settle. If these items indicated that some of his transactions were illegal, it could take years to move the will through the various courts. Her thoughts were interrupted when she heard Teresa calling her from downstairs. She hurriedly gathered everything and slid all of it under her bed.

"I hated to call you down here, but we have a problem in the yard," Teresa said. "There's a leak. Maybe a water line burst. Shall I call Greg?"

Mary Jo took her cell phone out of her pocket and said, "I'll do that. Thanks for letting me know. Hello, you two," she said as Otto and Walter came into the room.

Greg answered immediately, "Yeah?"

"There may be a water break in the yard. I can see little puddles of water from the fence line into the middle of the yard," Mary Jo explained.

"What next? I'll send someone right away. Do you think you could possibly stay out of trouble for a little while?" Greg said sarcastically.

"Greg, it's not my..." but Greg already had hung up.

"What's wrong?" Otto asked. Sensing that Mary Jo was upset, he instinctively put his arm around her shoulders.

"Don't let Walter go in the yard. We think there's a water main break. Someone will be here shortly to fix it. By the way, if you and Walter go upstairs to the balcony, you'll be able to watch the whole thing without getting wet," Mary Jo suggested.

It wasn't long before the plumber arrived with a low-boy, hauling a back hoe. Otto and Walter, with their faces pressed between the slats on the balcony, were entranced with the process involved in getting the back hoe into the yard.

Mary Jo waved to the plumber as she came out the back door. "Hi, Clyde," she called out.

"It's been a long time since I've seen you. I'm sorry about Roger," the friendly man said.

"Thank you. I think I'll watch for a while. I'm just as

curious as those two up there on the balcony," she said as she pointed to Otto and Walter.

"Well, those two are pals. If you see Otto, you can bet your bottom dollar that Walter's not too far behind," Clyde said as he climbed onto the back hoe.

When Clyde stopped the back hoe and walked over to the spot where he had been digging, Otto said to Walter, "He got too close to the rose bushes. I bet he hit the dead Indian. If he did, you're gonna see beautiful feathers because Indians liked to wear feathers in their hair. I saw pictures of them."

"I hit something," Clyde said to Mary Jo. As he looked down into the hole, he said, "It looks like a box."

"Roger's not going to like that they dug the Indian up," Otto whispered to Walter.

"Mary Jo, I'm going to take the lid off the box. It may be just filled with junk."

Mary Jo suddenly remembered the story of the dead Indian. Her concern now turned into fear. That was the spot where Otto told her that Walter was not to dig. She had thought Roger made up a story to entertain Otto. But, if something was buried there, it would mean that Roger knew all along that it was there.

Mary Jo was not the only one worried about what Clyde would find. Otto was holding his breath. He had never seen a dead body. He was surprised when the first thing that Clyde held up was a piece of cloth that looked just like the blanket Otto kept on his bed. At the same time, since there were no feathers, he was disappointed.

"Mary Jo, you better call the coroner. There's a pile of bones here. I'm not an expert, but I think they're human." Clyde then held up a piece of cloth that had brass buttons in a row.

"Walter, that's not an Indian. I know what's in there—Erik Danko, Roger's partner. He told me that Erik had a blanket just like mine. The buttons...the buttons look like the same kind that are on the jacket Roger gave me. Now, when I say my prayers tonight, I can tell Roger that I found his friend. He'll be very happy. Remember, Walter, this is a secret just between you and me."

Mary Jo dreaded that she had to call Greg once more. When he answered the phone, he said, "Now what?"

"You better get over here—the coroner's on his way."

"Mary Jo, if this is some kind of joke, I don't—"

"Shut up...this is serious. Clyde found a box and it contains what appears to be human bones. Now, damn it, get over here right away," Mary Jo ordered before she hung up the phone.

CHAPTER 43

ETH WAS PLEASED to see her dad's car parked in the driveway. After being away for so many weeks, she was delighted to be home again. While she loved backpacking in Australia with her friends, she was ready to settle down and begin her career with Fadden Insurance. Without getting her belongings out of her car, she raced up the front steps, flung the door open and yelled. "Hey, Dad, where are you hiding?" she shouted playfully. "Your little girl is home."

Greg hurriedly put his coffee cup down and rushed to the front door. His eyes opened wide when he saw a smiling Beth standing in the foyer. He wrapped his arms around his daughter. "Beth, baby, you're a sight to behold! Let me look at you...you're as lovely as ever."

"Dad, you really need to get glasses," Beth said as she smiled. "Where's Mom?"

"She's staying at Roger's home until we get some of the kinks worked out dealing with real estate and such with the will. Tell me, did you have a good time in Australia?" Greg said as he kept twirling Beth around to make sure that he wasn't dreaming.

"Dad, it was the best. But, gee, I was sorry I wasn't able to attend Papa Roger's funeral. I still can't believe he's gone. I did send him some emails while I was gone, and now I'm sure glad that I did. What's going to happen to Otto and Walter?"

"They'll be taken care of. We have to solve a myriad of legal problems first. I'll help you carry in your things from the car, and then you can take off to see your mom, if you'd like," Greg said, avoiding any talk of divorce.

"Dad, is everything alright between you and Mom?" Beth asked as she hung on to her dad's hand.

"Well, I'll let your mother handle that question, if you don't mind," Greg said, as the two of them starting unloading the trunk and carrying her belongings up the main staircase. When Beth opened her bedroom door, she said, "Oh, this looks sooooo good to me. While most of the places where we stayed overnight were fine, a couple of them left a lot to be desired," Beth stretched out across her bed and said, "Hello, bed," as she cuddled her pillows. "Dad, I'm going to shower and change before I leave."

"Okay, sweetie. I've got to attend a meeting at the bank, so I'll see you later," Greg said as he kissed her on the forehead. "Your Uncle Joshua is eager for you to begin your job with the company. He told me to tell you that he intends to chain you to your desk. I'd love to take you to dinner tonight if you would like, and I could probably get Joshua to go along. You know, it would give you time to get on the good side of your new boss," Greg said as he laughed.

After Beth had retrieved her backpack from her car, she rummaged through it and pulled out her cosmetic bag. "Dad, I'm going upstairs and get out of these clothes. I want to put on some soft, and silky."

When she neared her parents' bedroom, she decided to take a look inside. She was hoping that what her cousin Stella had texted her wasn't true. She couldn't imagine that they had separated. Feeling like an intruder, she looked around. Things were out of place. Then, she went into the bathroom. Pulling on the side of the medicine cabinet, she opened the door all the way. The only items in the cabinet were those belonging to her dad—nothing for her mom. She opened the closet door. The first thing that caught her eye was that her mom's neatly arranged shelves were now half empty. She stood there for a moment. Telling herself that her parents would never divorce, and that perhaps it would only be a temporary separation, she knew that she had to go see her mom immediately.

As she drove to Papa Roger's house, Beth was trying to sort out her feelings. To think of her mom with someone else was still foreign to her. *Who could it be? Were they serious? I lost Papa Roger and now I may be losing my parents as a couple. If they no longer love each other, they may not love me.* She spotted her mom sitting on one of the steps at the front door, while Otto and Walter were rolling around on the grass playing with a rope.

When Otto saw her, he jumped up and ran to her car. Otto stood by shyly until Beth reached for him. Then, he smiled and hugged her back. "Walter, say hello to Beth," Otto said. Walter stood with his nose tight against Beth's leg, waiting to be petted.

After Otto was certain that Walter had received proper recognition, he said, "Come now, Walter, we have work to do. We have sidewalks to sweep and trash to remove. See you later," Otto said as he led Walter down the sidewalk, heading for town.

"Come in, sweetheart. You look fabulous," Mary Jo said as she headed for the living room.

"Mom, I know something's wrong," Beth said as she sat

down beside her mom. "Stella told me that you and Dad are separated. When I questioned him, he told me to ask you."

Mary Jo took Beth's hands in hers. "This is probably one of the hardest things that I probably will ever have to tell you. Yes, your dad and I have separated. It was all my fault. You see, Beth, I was unhappy and lonely. However, that doesn't justify what I did." Mary Jo paused and looked away. She knew that she had to tell Beth everything. "I was unfaithful. I had an affair with a man I met while working with the STAIRS program. I can't explain why I did it. I only know that it was my fault. Your father did nothing to deserve my behavior. I've asked him to forgive me, but he's very angry. He feels betrayed and I can't blame him. Perhaps he will forgive me some day. I know this affects you, too. So, I'm asking for your forgiveness."

"Mom, you don't need my forgiveness. Are you two certain that you want a divorce? You know, sometimes these things can be worked out," Beth said hopefully.

"I've ended the affair. But, yes, there will be a divorce. Beth, I want to be on my own and learn who I'm supposed to be. While it's a little late in my life for an analysis, I know that I have to do this. It may take time for your Uncle Joshua and your father to get everything straightened out with Roger's estate, so I may have to stay here for some time. However, when the time comes for me to move, I'll be getting a place. Your dad and I agreed that you're to choose where you want to call home. However, I'll file for divorce. Beth, please don't hate me."

"Mom, I could never hate you or Dad. You're my parents. I want both of you to be happy. I wish we could all go back to the way it was, but I'm old enough to know that life doesn't always work that way."

Just then the doorbell chimed. "I'll get it, Mom," Beth said as she went to the front door. "Oh, hi, Uncle Joshua. We were just talking about you," Beth said as she gave her uncle a hug.

"What are you doing tomorrow night?" Joshua asked.

"Why, what's up?" Beth replied.

As he walked into the kitchen, Joshua said, "I purchased a full table for the STAIRS Ball. I've already invited Cindy and Russ." He then turned to Mary Jo. "They'll be picking Otto up since they want you to be alone with Mitch," Joshua said lightheartedly.

"Mitch? You mean Mitch from the animal sanctuary?" Beth asked.

"That's the one," Joshua said.

"Oh, that Cindy," Mary Jo said, "she's trying to be a matchmaker. "I already told Mitch that I'll go with him, but don't read anything into it. We both must be there since our charities are part of STAIRS. But wait until Otto hears that he's going to the dance, too. I better check to see if his black suit needs to be pressed."

"Beth, are you ready to start your new job Monday a week?" Joshua asked. "I've called a meeting of the Fadden Insurance and Real Estate offices in the eastern half of the state," Joshua explained. "After you pass your one-year trial period, you'll receive a promotion to assistant Tri-County Manager."

"Uncle Joshua, I'm thrilled to get this opportunity. I'll do my best to make you proud. Could I please have Papa Roger's desk when I get an office?"

"It's upstairs in his study. You mean to say that you like that old, ornate thing?" Joshua asked.

"Papa Roger used to play office with me when I was a kid. I would pretend that I was a customer. One time—oh, this is cute—one time I asked to buy insurance for my turtle. Papa Roger asked me why I wanted insurance. I told him that since the turtle was my best friend, I didn't want him to crawl out of my yard and leave me. So, he sold me insurance for a quarter. I then asked him if *he* had a best friend. He proclaimed that the river was his best friend. I told him that he needed insurance, too, so Timber Run River would always protect him. Then, I sold *him* insurance for a quarter. Later, when I told him that the turtle was no longer in my yard, he declared that I was lucky since I had insurance. He paid me dollar. I can still see him reaching into his desk drawer and pulling out a crisp one dollar bill." She paused as she remembered those precious moments. "I was happy with the dollar, but I really wanted the turtle back," Beth said. "So, may I have the desk?"

CHAPTER 44

M ARY JO WAS looking forward to the Ball tonight, especially since Beth was going along. She knew the news about the bones was still running rampant throughout the community, but that was to be expected. As she slipped on her strapless, ankle-length, black taffeta gown, and stepped into her rhinestone heels, she was starting to get her mind wrapped around having a good time tonight—bones or no bones.

Checking her watch, she hurried down the steps just as the doorbell rang. Opening the door, she was delighted when she got her first glimpse at Mitch.

"Mitch, how handsome you look tonight. I'll be the envy of all the women," she teased as he came through the front door.

"All I can say is that I clean up very well. But you, my lady, look amazing," he said as he handed her a corsage box. "I know I'm supposed to pin this on you, but, Mary Jo, how do I do that?" he asked, as he looked at her bare shoulders.

Mary Jo took the box, removed a white orchid and pinned it on her dress. As Otto and Walter came scampering up the basement steps and into the dining room, Mary Jo said, "Otto, you look very nice in your suit and you chose a perfect tie. Cindy and Russ will be stopping here to pick you up in a half hour. You realize that Walter can't go with you to the Ball."

"Oh, he knows. I explained it to him," Otto said confidently.

"Alright, then, we'll see you there shortly," Mary Jo said as she left with Mitch.

When Mary Jo saw the shiny black Corvette parked in the driveway, she asked, "What happened to your truck?"

"I couldn't take the prettiest girl in town to the Ball in a pick-up. I only rented it for tonight," Mitch explained. And since I lack the proper Irish magic to turn a pumpkin into a Corvette, I imposed upon our local car rental company. So, m'lady, we have this sporty chariot for the whole, glorious evening."

Mitch smiled at Mary Jo and she found herself relaxing. As he helped her get into the car, she thought, "God, he's so warm, so thoughtful, and so appealing. It's impossible not to like him. He's definitely charming and attractive—yes, that was it—attractive— especially those blue eyes.

The ride to the Ball was filled with pleasant small talk and gentle humor. As they pulled into the parking lot, Mitch said, "Oh, my newest guests have arrived. The twin baby donkeys appear to like their new home and they settled in quickly."

The ballroom was a sight to behold. There were greens and flowers everywhere. The ceiling was covered with sparkling lights, coming as close to resembling the nighttime skies as possible. On each table for eight was a bowl of flowers surrounded with small LED lights in little crystal holders. Ushers were escorting people to their reserved seats while a pianist played soft music.

"This is elegant!" Mary Jo said. "I really didn't expect to see something so lovely here in this humongous space."

Suddenly, Crystal was at her side. She was wearing a black sequined form-fitting Holston, with a plunging neckline—a perfect setting to show off her genuine diamond earrings. Her long hair was arranged in a chignon. "My God, Mary Jo, whose body did they find? Did you see it? What did it look like?" an excited Crystal asked.

"No, I did not see a body. I saw pieces of cloth. I also did not see the bones, and, no, I don't know if there was a body buried there or not," Mary Jo said, trying to placate Crystal so she would leave.

"Well, I must run along. Sinclair will be looking for me," she said as she hurried away.

For a split second, Mary Jo spied Greg heading across the room. He seemed to be alone. She had hoped that he would bring a date—perhaps just to make her feel less guilty. When Cindy, Russ and Otto appeared, Mary Jo felt that she could have lit a candle with Otto's smile. He shook hands with everyone.

"How's Walter?" Mitch asked.

"He's fine. I explained why he had to stay at home. I bought him a new toy this morning just to make him feel better," Otto said. "Will I be sitting at this table?"

"Yes, you will. But until dinner is announced, Otto, you may walk around and meet and greet others. Have fun," Mary Jo said as Otto practically skipped away.

As Mary Jo watched Otto greet a group of guests, a voice behind her whispered, "Crystal's wearing Halston. I bet it cost a thousand bucks!" Mary Jo recognized Cindy's voice immediately and motioned for her to sit down.

"How do you know?"

"Because I saw a film star being interviewed at the awards show the other night on TV. She had on that very dress," Cindy huffed.

Mary Jo and Cindy critically watched Crystal share a glass of champagne with Sinclair. Cindy then said, "Okay, anything new?"

"No. The bones have been shipped to some state forensic agency. I just want all of this to go away," Mary Jo said as she squeezed Cindy's hand.

"It will take time. So, my recommendation for tonight is to just tell those who ask about the bones that nothing is new. But, more importantly, just relax and have a good time. Russ is getting us some wine and dinner will be in about an hour. Get ready, sweetie, here comes Gertrude, the biggest gossip in the entire state," Cindy warned as she laughed.

"Mary Jo, you poor, poor dear. What a horrible thing to happen to such a lovely lady," Gertrude gushed. "Imagine, having a dead body in your back yard. *Dreadful!* I was shocked when I found out that you're staying in Roger's home. Aren't you lonely there? But then, Roger's no longer here. Who's going to inherit that lovely home? I hope you're bearing up under all this."

"I'm fine. The coroner is handling the problem. Oh, someone's waving for me. I'll see you later. Have a good time," Mary Jo said as she scooted away.

Cindy chuckled. Gertrude stood there for a moment, but, finally, she clucked, "The poor dear—how she must be suffering. Oh, there's Otto. I'll see what he knows."

The dinner bell rang and, in no time at all, everyone was seated. Mayor Pendleton welcomed the guests and thanked the pianist for providing music. After he provided a short history on how STAIRS was formed and gave accolades to all the participating charities, he expressed condolences to the Fadden family on the loss of their patriarch. He reminded everyone that Roger Fadden's extreme generosity would make tomorrow's opening ceremony so very special. Lastly, he turned the mic over to Dr. Howard, who provided grace.

"Mitch, I hear you arrived in a Corvette. How'd you like it?" Russ asked.

"It was a rush. I'd love to take it out on the highway and see what *she* would do and how *she* would handle" Mitch said jovially. "However, I think Mary Jo likes the pick-up better."

As Mitch and Russ discussed the merits of sports cars, Otto leaned over and whispered into Mary Jo's ear, "Mary Jo, everyone's asking me about the bones. What should I say?"

"What *did* you say?" she asked patiently.

"I said I didn't see a body and I didn't see any bones. I know the secret, but I promised Roger that I wouldn't tell," Otto said convincingly.

"You said the right thing, Otto. Whatever was found was probably buried there a long time ago. Now, we have a new rule tonight—no more talk about bones. Otto, don't forget to save me a dance," Mary Jo said to a blushing Otto.

When Mitch turned to Mary Jo and extended his hand, he said, "May I have this dance, lovely lady?"

It was then that the evening took an unexpected turn for Mary Jo. When she felt Mitch's hand at her waist, a feeling of excitement surged through her body. It frightened her a bit. Her first thought was that it was too early to feel this way—she recently had made a terrible mistake—but this feeling was one of comfort and seemed natural.

"Do you have any idea how long I have waited to hold you like this?" Mitch whispered in her ear.

Instinctively, she squeezed his hand. "I must take this slowly, Mitch. I'm terrified, but, at the same time, I know we're going to be alright," Mary Jo said as she laid her head on his shoulder and relaxed for the first time in months.

When they returned to their table, Mitch thought it would be a good time to ask Beth to dance. He wanted to demonstrate that he had good manners. "Beth, may I have this dance?" he asked with a slight tremor in his voice.

"Certainly. I'd love to."

Just as Mary Jo turned to watch her daughter and Mitch, Greg was at her side. "Is *he* the new man?" he sneered.

Russ was watching the scene unfurl. "Mary Jo, I believe this is my dance," he said as he took her hand and led her away from the table.

"You're still taking care of her, aren't you?" Greg snarled to Cindy as he turned and walked away.

CHAPTER 45

It was opening day for STAIRS, and the sidewalks in Riverton were lined with all types of chairs to save front row spots for the big parade. Mary Jo, however, had left for the sanctuary at dawn in order to help take the animals to the park. Mitch had rounded up a dozen residents, who were willing to help position the ark and to make walking areas for some of the animals. Mary Jo was in charge of signage and the *Take an Animal to Lunch* applications that the children would be filling out. Municipal workers were busy arranging folding chairs in front of the amphitheater, where the US Army Band would be playing after the parade.

Otto was extremely excited. When the twin baby donkeys were released in a fenced-off area, he tied bright purple ribbons around their necks. Using his brand new phone, he started snapping photos. He moved from one animal to another, talking with them and helping with the fencing.

"Mary Jo, are the kids really gonna take an animal to lunch? How are they gonna do that?"

"The children will be donating money for their favorite animal to have lunch at the sanctuary where they live. On each animal's permanent enclosure, there will be a list of the names of the children who are helping to feed that animal. It's somewhat like adopting them, except they can't take the animal home. The children will be encouraged to visit their animal frequently. In addition, each child may submit names for the baby donkeys. Maybe Mitch will let you draw the winning name out of the barrel. Wouldn't that be fun?" Mary Jo suggested.

Gloria, from Davis Media, arrived with five workers. "Mitch, we're here to help in any way we can. With the size of the crowd that's already assembling for the parade, you'll be swamped. We brought along tables and chairs that you can use for registration. We also have velvet ropes and poles to create a path so the children will get to see all the animals and not step on one another. We're all yours for the day," Gloria said as she began to check out the animals. "By the way, how long do you think the parade's going to last?"

"It's scheduled to start at nine and end around twelve," Mary Jo replied. "Look at Cleopatra! She loves the feel of the grass under her feet. I'm amazed at how well she gets around with that one short leg. She sure is frisky for a goat. Otto, do you have any more ribbons? I think Cleopatra would appreciate a bow."

"Can I put one on the Professor?" Otto asked as he pointed to the white owl.

Mitch laughed. "No, Otto, he wouldn't like that. He doesn't like anyone to touch his wings. He can't really fly—he simply flutters from one spot to another. But, you could put one on the outside of his temporary enclosure."

"I'm gonna put a red bow on Sir Galahad. While I know he's blind and can't see, I think he would like to look handsome for the children. He's such a pretty little horse," Otto stated as he shook his head up and down. "Romeo, that pretty peacock, brought his own fancy feathers to show the children. He doesn't need any ribbons. Just look at how he likes to show off his feathers."

Meanwhile, the crowd was lined up on Hemlock to see the parade. Promptly at nine, the festivities began with the United States Army Band leading the way. People were clapping and waving their hats in the air. The Riverton High School Band was next, followed by dozens of majorettes. Twenty floats, each vying for the prize for the best float in the parade, were interspersed with marching bands from the schools all over the county. Much to the delight of the viewers, antique cars from all over the state also made an appearance. The riding club received a hand as they marched down the street with their horses dressed in their finery. It seemed that every club for miles around wanted to join in the STAIRS celebration.

Shortly after noon, the crowd began moving to the park. As soon as the children spotted the animals, they shouted with delight. Gloria helped to quiet the children down by lining them up along the entrance way. Mitch marveled at the way she helped to bring some order to what could have been chaos. Mary Jo helped the children fill out their application as well as the names for the baby donkeys.

Gloria approached Mitch and whispered, "That's Jacob Weber over there," she said as her eyes indicated a well-dressed older man, who was carrying a little girl in his arms.

"And he is...?" Mitch asked.

"You're familiar with Jacob's Goods, aren't you?"

"Oh, the big chain store that has the slogan *"Tomorrow's Goods Today"*.

"Get over there and introduce yourself," Gloria said as she gave Mitch a gentle shove in the right direction.

"And who do we have here?" Mitch asked as he took the

little girl's hand. It was then that he noticed her disability. Just then Mary Jo joined the group.

"This little bundle is Geraldine, my granddaughter," Jacob said as he kissed the toddler on the head.

"My name is Geri, but Grandpop calls me Geraldine," she said proudly.

"What a pretty name," Mary Jo said. As she turned to Jacob Weber, she said, "Would it be alright if I took Geraldine over to meet Sir Galahad? He's very tame and he loves to have little girls make a fuss over him."

Jacob handed Geraldine over to Mary Jo. "She couldn't wait to get here to see the animals. She was awake at the crack of dawn. By the way, I'm Jacob Weber. You must be Mitch McCabe. Ever since Darius Davis told me about your sanctuary, my mind's been racing on how Jacob's Goods could participate with you in a meaningful partnership."

Mitch was speechless. He thought that Darius forgot all about his promise to find a corporate sponsor for his animals.

Gloria spoke up. "Mr. Weber, I had the pleasure of hearing you speak at the National Advertisers Conference last month. Mitch has been doing a yeoman's job trying to take care of the throw-away animals on his own. We could set up a meeting between you two sometime next week if you're still going to be in this area."

"As a matter of fact, I'll be here until the end of the month. You see," he whispered, "Geraldine must have another operation."

Mary Jo returned with Geraldine, who was really excited about naming the baby donkeys. "Grandpop, I want to call them *Honey* and *Sugar*. My daddy calls my mama *Honey* and she calls him *Sugar*. Can we buy them? I have lots of money in my piggy bank."

"Well, we can't take them home, sweetie, but Grandpop can help to make them more comfortable. We can come back every once in a while to visit them. How about that?"

"Oh, you are such a good Grandpop," Geraldine then kissed him.

The afternoon went by very quickly for Otto. Before he knew it, Mitch announced that it was five o'clock—time to draw the names for the donkeys. "Otto, put your hand in the barrel and mix up the slips—that's it. Now, pick just one slip and hand it to me."

Otto took his time. He loved being the center of attention. He moved his arm around and around. Then, he said, "One, two, three," and chose one slip.

"Hey, little fellows, you now have names." As he held onto the donkey that was handicapped, he said, "Little man, your name is *Mike*." Then he held onto the other donkey, and said, "From now on you will be called *Ike*."

"*Ike* and *Mike*, *Ike* and *Mike*," the children shouted.

Mitch realized that he was going to have some difficulty closing down his exhibit. The band had vacated about two hours before, but the children showed no interest in saying goodbye to the animals. However, one by one, Mitch and his helpers were able to put the animals back in the ark. The truck that would haul it to the sanctuary was finally able to hitch up to the ark. As the children waved goodbye, calling out the animals' names, then, and only then did the remaining children bother to look for their parents.

Otto and Walter were in Mary Jo's car, waiting for her to drive them home. "Walter, wasn't this the bestest day ever and ever? What fun we had!"

"Okay, guys. You two did a great job. Walter, the next two days you'll be able to wear your red cape and your top hat as you welcome children who come to see David's Dancing Dogs. Otto, you must make sure that Walter gets a good sleep so he can be bright-eyed and bushy-tailed for his job."

Otto wrinkled his brows and looked at Mary Jo. "How can Walter's tail get bushy? And, he has only one eye. They never change," Otto stated solemnly.

Mary Jo laughed. "You're right, Otto. He'll be as handsome as ever."

⋙ CHAPTER 46 ⋘

IVERTON HAD NEVER played host to so many tourists. All the hotels had been fully booked and the restaurants were doing a booming business. Perfect strangers were having a blast as they moved from one event to another. Among the locals, word was spreading about the bones that had been found in Roger Fadden's back lawn the other day. As the story was repeated from one group to another, the story grew exponentially. By the time the four-day event was over, the rumor mill claimed that there were dozens and dozens of bones found, along with several skulls.

A group of four men, wearing ribbons across their chests that said **HOST,** were stopping people, who were walking from one event to another, to survey them about their STAIRS experience. Darius Davis had finally come out of his self-imposed imprisonment and was actually enjoying speaking to the visitors. He had agreed to help since he felt that any data they might gather would be helpful if the committee decided to repeat the charity drive in a few years. Darius knew where Mary Jo would be, so he purposefully avoided those events. After that day when she had ordered him out of her car, he hadn't try to contact her—he knew that such a move would be dangerous for him.

Gloria had called him last evening to tell him about Jacob Weber and his interest in Mitch's animal sanctuary. He realized that Mary Jo might not ever know that he was the one who had suggested to Weber that he should look into choosing the sanctuary as one of his corporate charities. He had promised Mitch that he would try to find a sponsor. Perhaps it would be better if she didn't know. He didn't trust himself to see her. He must stay away. Now he realized what it was like to love someone whom he could never have. He thought he knew how to play the little game so well—he had his family—and, when he wanted, he had Mary Jo. The game came back and bit him in his ass.

"Hello, folks," Darius said to a middle-aged couple. "May I ask you a few questions?"

"Sure. But I don't want to be late for the swim meet. Our son is competing," the man said.

Darius checked his list. "That meet begins in an hour. The YMCA is right around the corner. Are you folks from out of town?"

"Yes, we're from Philly."

"Welcome. What events have you attended so far, and what are your comments about the presentations?" Darius asked.

"I attended the Belly Dancing Lessons," the woman giggled. "It was so much fun. And tonight we're going to hear the gospel singers."

He then stopped a group of tourists who seemed eager to talk with him. However, they jumped in right away with questions about the bones that had been found. One very excited man said that he thought the story about someone finding bones was only a rumor to entertain the tourists.

"No, it wasn't a rumor. As far as I know," Darius said as he smiled, "they have not identified the bones, yet. But I did hear that it appeared that they had been buried there for years and years."

"Wow, imagine having bones in your yard! That's scary," a woman wearing a floppy straw hat said.

"Can you folks tell me about the events you have seen so far?" Darius asked, anxious to get back on track. "We're eager to get your opinions."

"It's the first time I ever saw an arm wrestling contest," one man said. "But what I really liked was the team trivia contest. While we didn't win, we enjoyed participating. And, I thought the prizes were fantastic. You people did a great job with this whole idea of a charity week."

"From a woman's point of view, the sessions on makeup as well as the one on flower arranging were very informative. I'd recommend that you do this every year. Oh, and you have such unusual things for sale. I bought this straw hat at a little stand over by the Riverton Farm Show building, where we went to see David's Dancing Dogs. They were so cute."

"I attended Professor Woolls' lecture on Climate Warming. He certainly was knowledgeable. And, tomorrow, I'm going to walk a dog. And I just may do that again on Friday. That will give me two chances to win a free vacation."

Darius immediately thought about Mary Jo. He needed to get himself under control. It was all his idea that their affair had started in the first place. At first, he had thought it would be just a flirtation—nothing too serious. When it became much more than that, he was convinced that he could manage both a family and a mistress. He hadn't given any thought to what Mary Jo had expected. He had just assumed that his wife would never discover his affair, and if she did, he could easily talk his way out of any trouble. He always had before. However, Mary Jo had no intention of remaining the other woman. It was at her insistence that the affair ended.

Darius hurried to his car, tossed his paperwork inside, and

drove away. As he looked in his rearview mirror, he told himself that he must put all thoughts of Mary Jo in the back of his mind. He must take care of his children and that meant that he also must stay with his wife—at least for now.

Meanwhile, Otto and Walter were welcoming guests to see David's Dancing Dogs at the farm show building. Walter was wearing the bright red cape and the black top hat that Mary Jo had helped Otto buy online. Otto was strutting around, much like he had seen the peacock do the other day. And, all four shows were sold out.

The next two days were as busy and lucrative as the first two. Visitors shopped, ate, particpated in activities, and generously opened their wallets. The STAIRS Committee was sure that the last two days were more crowded than the first. They speculated that "word of mouth" had made a difference.

Cindy was busy each of the four days, registering people who were willing to pay fifty dollars to walk a dog from the Cutler County Animal Rescue Association. As a reward, each walker was given a lottery ticket that would be entered into a drawing for free vacation trips. Cindy was thrilled that a side benefit resulted in five dogs being adopted by their walkers.

As the week drew to a close, the STAIRS Committee was already congratulating themselves on a successful event. While a meeting was scheduled for the following week to debrief each charity on the total income raised, predictions were being made that it would be over a million dollars.

As tourists began to clear out of Riverton, the town began to look normal once again. The administrators of the different charities could not have been more pleased with the results of the STAIRS program. However, the residents of the little city beside the river would be the real winners since the funds for increasing vital services were now available.

CHAPTER 47

As Mary Jo opened her eyes early in the morning and glanced out the window, she was surprised to see thick fog. The weather had been beautiful for the entire four days of their charity drive. However, for some reason, she had always felt uneasy in fog. Was it because she had read too many mystery novels, where scary creatures emerged from the fog and caused havoc? Or, did the fog simply remind her that she felt lost in a sea of decisions that she had to make? Either way, it left her with an errie feeling.

Shaking her head a bit as if to clear the fog out of her brain, she realized that she had an extremely important decision to make—what to do about the items that were in a shoebox under her bed. She felt ashamed for lying to Otto after he had trusted her by showing her the secret drawer. It only made it harder for her to decide what she should do with the items she now had in her possession.

While she didn't think any of the items were connected to the bones found in the back lawn, several notations worried her. One pack of index cards had the words *Hialeah* and *Vinnie* on one line and $2,500 on another. Slipping the rubber band off another pack marked *Little Vinnie—Bronx,* she found several strange cards: one with HGK—AVK63943000863211 and one that said Hong Kong—1.5M: $560,000.

Another pack that had cards which looked extremely strange bore a label that said; Universal Sea Capital LTD—along with one that said: Antwerp—Grote Markt—Otto or Willem. Could this mean that Roger was up to his neck in illegal dealings? Could these cards have been in that drawer before Roger bought the desk? But he knew they were there—he had shown them to Otto. Who was she kidding! Roger knew—he knew! Perhaps she should just let sleeping dogs lie.

However, since Mary Jo had recently learned that Beth had asked her Uncle Joshua for Roger's old desk, she needed to tell Beth just in case there were other things hidden in that damned desk.

Just as she finished making her bed, she heard Beth's voice. "Mom," Beth shouted up the staircase, "come out, come out, wherever you are." Beth used the words that Mary Jo had used when they had played Hide and Seek so many years ago. "I brought buns. Hurry. I'll put on the coffee."

Mary Jo quickly shoved the shoebox under the bed and hurried down the steps. Soon they were seated at the kitchen table, chatting about the events of the past few days. "I never saw so many people walking the streets of our little town. It was such fun. I spent a bundle, but I had a great time," Beth said as she carried their empty cups to the kitchen sink.

"Now I have a surprise to show you, my precious one," Mary Jo said as she smiled at Beth. "Follow me."

"This sounds mysterious. Where are you taking me?"

"Up to your desk," Mary Jo said as Beth followed her up the staircase. She opened the door to Roger's den and pointed to the ornate walnut desk in the center of the room. "Come with me and watch carefully."

When Mary Jo touched the Indian carving and the drawer popped open, Beth jumped.

"Oh, snap," Beth said. "How did you know about that?"

"Otto showed me. He had promised Roger that he wouldn't tell anyone about the drawer. When the drawer opened, I was shocked to see several packs of index cards with cryptic remarks. I have them in my room," Mary Jo explained.

Beth was on the floor, examining the drawer. When she tried to close it, she stopped. "Mom, it feels as if there's something stuck in the back of the drawer. You may have missed something. Hand me the ruler that's alongside the lamp."

Beth began to slide the ruler back and forth. "Yep, there's something there. I think...now wait...I think there's more than one thing. It's good I have long arms," Beth giggled. "Here we go. I have them. Mom, look, two cell phones."

Mary Jo's heart fell. My God, this might even be worse than the items she already had. "Come with me, honey," Mary Jo said as they hurried to her room. She reached under the bed, retrieved the shoebox, and then spread everything over the quilt.

At first, Beth was almost motionless. Then, she began to pick up the various index cards to examine them closely. "Mom, what does all this mean?"

"I'm not sure. But I don't think it's good. I've been trying to decide if I should turn all this over to Detective Fulbright. But I'm concerned what it might mean to Greg, Joshua and, especially, you What if Roger was involved in something illegal?"

Beth was lying across the bottom of the bed, aimlessly tracing the patterns in the quilt with her fingers. She most certainly knew right from wrong. But this involved her Papa Roger.

"My Papa Roger was good and kind. Many people are

involved in things that are not legal—so what," Beth said forlornly. "Can't we just throw all this away?"

"We can't do that," Mary Jo argued. "I know I should turn this stuff in, but I just can't bring myself to do it."

Beth thought awhile. "Mom, if you'd like, I'll do it," Beth said.

Mary Jo put all the items back in the shoebox, tied a ribbon around it, and handed it to Beth.

As Beth stood up, she said, "Look, Mom, the fog is gone. That's a good sign."

"Mary Jo," Teresa called up the staircase.

"Yes, Teresa, what is it?"

"The police are holding a press conference about someone from Riverton, who was murdered. I thought you'd like to know."

"Thank you, Teresa," Mary Jo said as she hurriedly turned her TV on. Detective Fulbright was handing a microphone to a woman. "My name is Hilda Henderson. My brother Henry lived in Riverton for several years. He was a private detective." She paused briefly, then, in a shaky voice, she went on, "He was murdered in Pittsburgh right before Christmas. If anyone knows why Henry was in Pittsburgh at that time, or if you can help us in any way, please contact Detective Fulbright. I loved by brother very much."

"Mom, what's wrong?" Beth asked.

"Sweetie, I'm not sure. I don't know if Roger knew this man, but it gives me the creeps just to think about him," Mary Jo replied.

"But even if Papa Roger knew this Henry, that doesn't mean he had anything to do with his murder," Beth emphasized.

"I know. I know. Call it *intuition*. Call me crazy, but it scares me."

"Mom, I can turn that shoebox in for you. You're upset. Right now things are not great between you and Dad. I understand that you don't want to make them worse, so let me take the cards and the phones to Detective Fulbright," Beth said.

"I appreciate your offer. Let me sleep on this. I'll let you know in the morning what I want to do. You're so very precious to me, my darling daughter. You know, Teresa told me that Roger had been shredding lots of paperwork and had filled several trash bags that he had put out on the curb. So, I cannot imagine why he didn't shred this stuff, too. I imagine that he thought that he had plenty of time to do just that. Now, let's forget about all this tonight and have a wonderful dinner."

Chapter 48

WHEN MARY JO joined Beth in the kitchen for breakfast, Beth had her nose buried in the morning paper. "Mom, did you know that Jacob's is going to open a store on Maple Drive? I love that store. They always have such neat things."

"Well, did you know that Jacob Weber, the owner, will be providing the financing needed to improve and enhance Mitch's animal sanctuary? It all sounds good to me."

"Wow. I bet Mitch is excited about that. Now, as far as our little shoebox is concerned, Mom—do you want me to take it to Detective Fulbright?" Beth asked.

"Yes. I think it will work out better if you deliver it," Mary Jo said as she poured herself another cup of coffee.

A few minutes later, Beth walked out the front door and drove directly to the Riverton Police Department parking lot. She sat there awhile, thinking over what she was about to do. She was still resisting the thought that her Papa Roger knew all along what had happened to his partner. Then, she remembered the show she had watched last night, where the police were able to retrieve damning evidence against someone simply by finding all the calls he had received or sent on his cell phone. Suddenly, she pulled the ribbon on the shoebox, took out the cell phones, and then retied the ribbon.

She walked up the front steps and opened the door. Holding the shoebox in her arms, she approached the front desk.

"I would like to see Detective Fulbright."

"Follow me, Miss," a jovial policeman directed.

She was pleasantly surprised to see such a handsome man. "How may I help you," Fulbright said as he gave her a big smile.

"My name is Beth Fadden. I'm delivering this shoebox for my mother, Mary Jo Fadden."

"Won't you sit down?" Fulbright said as he pulled out a chair for her.

"We found these items in Roger Fadden's desk. However, we're not certain that they belonged to him. They could have been there when he purchased the desk."

As he took a quick look inside the shoebox, he said, "I see." Fulbright then took a few seconds to look at the beautiful woman sitting beside his desk. "The Faddens have cooperated with us, and we'll do our best to keep you updated on any progress we make. You never know what clues we might find to help us identify the bones that were found in Mr. Fadden's lawn. Ms. Fadden, may I have your phone number?"

Beth raised an eyebrow. "Of course." As she provided her number, she didn't fail to notice that Fulbright was flushed.

In a few minutes, it was over. She had given the shoebox to the handsome Detective Fulbright. As she walked to her car, Beth couldn't stop smiling. The ball is in his court—but I do hope that he calls me strictly on his own.

Then Beth drove to Hemlock Street and parked her car. She walked across the street and sat down on the bench that Papa Roger loved so much. She accepted the possibility that he might have made money on financial deals that the government didn't know about. However, she was certain that he would not have been involved in murder. Her concentration was broken when she heard a voice behind her.

"Hi, Beth," Otto said as he led Walter to the bench where he sat down.

"Hello, Otto. You, too, Walter," Beth said as she scooted over to give Otto more room. "How have you two been?"

"I'm still so sad. I miss Roger. He was my friend. He was supposed to get a ride in a big, big truck next week with Russ. Roger told me since I was part of his tended family, I could go along," Otto said proudly.

"Tended family? Oh, you probably mean extended family."

"Yeah, that's what he said, but I don't know if that's good or bad."

"That's very good, Otto. It means that, even though you were not born into the Fadden family, we consider you one of us," Beth explained.

"That makes me happy. Walter and I come here every day to talk with Roger. Do you think he hears us?" Otto said as he picked Walter up and put him on his lap.

"Yes, I do. Papa Roger liked you a lot, Otto. And, surprisingly, he also liked Walter," Beth said as she chuckled.

"Do you know that Roger liked you the best?" Otto asked.

"How do you know that?"

"Cause the only picture on his big, big desk was one of you sitting on a pony," Otto responded. "And that means he really, really liked you."

"What do you talk about with Papa Roger?"

"Oh, I told him that I found his partner, Erik."

Beth sat up straight. "You did! Where?"

"Oh, one day some guy found bones in a box buried near the rose bushes," Otto said proudly. "Inside there was gold buttons and a piece of a blanket, too. Roger gave me a jacket with the same kind of gold buttons. He told me Erik and him used to wear them in Civil War enactments. And, he gived me a blanket—the same kind that he gived to Erik. I have mine on my bed. So, I told Roger that someone had put Erik in that box. Now he knows where he is."

It took a few minutes for Beth to digest the information that Otto had just given her. When she realized that Papa Roger knew all the time what had happened to Erik, she could hardly breathe. That would mean either Roger put him there or he knew who did—*she didn't want to go there.* "My God. My God," Beth said as she closed her eyes.

"Beth, are you praying?" Otto asked.

Beth knew that she had to get control of herself. "Yes, Otto, I am."

"Will you ask God to look after Roger? I want to be sure that he is alright," Otto said as he stood up. "Walter, it's time we start our job. Let's go," Otto said as he patted Walter on the head. "Bye, Beth, see you later, alligator," Otto said as he walked away laughing hard.

Staring at the rapidly moving river, Beth was trying to determine what she was going to do next. She loved Papa Roger. She still loved him. But, if he really committed such a heinous crime, he should be punished. How does one punish a dead man? Does the public need to know about his crime? It won't change anything—or will it?

She fingered the cell phones in her pocket. One option would be to take them to Fulbright—another would be to toss them into the river. She stood up and slowly walked down to the river's edge. If she knew that some other person had committed this crime, why would it be easier to turn these damned phones over to the police? She thought about the Ten Commandments. Papa Roger certainly knew about them, too.

Nearing the river's turn, she reached in her pocket and pulled out one of the phones. Raising her arm up in the air, she pulled it back, but almost immediately changed her mind and fell to her knees. She wept.

It was deathly quiet. Even the birds had stopped chirping. Just then, the sound of an ambulance, zooming down Hemlock Street, made her shiver. She stood up. Slowly, she had returned to reality. She had made her decision. Love won out. Clutching the phones in her hand and grateful that the current was rapid, she tossed them into the river.

"Papa Roger, you're lucky that you bought insurance from me. Just like my turtle's insurance, yours paid off, too."

EPILOGUE (2 YEARS LATER)

➤ Mary Jo and Mitch celebrated their first wedding anniversary. They frequently enjoy lunch in a little gazebo that Mitch built down by the riverside, where they remind one another how lucky they are that they met and fell in love.

➤ The wealthy widow Crystal Hancock is on the prowl for Husband Number Three.

➤ Walter, the ugly but lovable dog, passed away of old age. Three months later, Otto died. Everyone assumed that Otto died of a broken heart.

➤ Darius came home from a business trip to an almost empty house. All that was left was a table, a chair, a bowl, a knife and fork, and a note—*this house is as empty as your heart.*

➤ On the anniversary of his death, the Riverton Chamber of Commerce dedicated the bench along Timber Run River to Roger Fadden.

➤ Joshua Fadden married Morgan Truesdale in Las Vegas. As a wedding gift to Morgan, Joshua presented him with the keys to their new home—Roger Fadden's mansion.

➤ Greg Fadden now lives in Hamilton Haven, former home of Sarah McIntyre, and is considered one of Riverton's most eligible bachelors.

➤ Jacob Weber honored the promise he had made to his granddaughter, Geraldine, to support the animal sanctuary by building a modern, spacious animal habitat. It is now recognized as a model for the nation.

➤ Beth Fadden and Detective Fulbright are engaged to be married.

➤ A little shoebox, stored in the Evidence Room at police headquarters, had fallen behind a loose board of paneling during renovations. It was never seen again.

➤ The newly-elected District Attorney for Clinton County created a Cold Case Department. He announced that both the case of the bones found in Roger Fadden's lawn as well as a joint assignment with the Pittsburgh Police Department, regarding the murder of Henry Henderson, will be reopened.

Printed in the United States
By Bookmasters